Reviews adore

SHARIE KOHLER

and the novels in her exhilarating
Moon Chasers series!

"Do not miss this next exciting story in the thrilling Moon Chasers series."
—Fresh Fiction on *My Soul to Keep*

"Readers are in for an incredible ride."
—Romantic Times on *To Crave a Blood Moon*

"Sparks fly and the attraction sizzles . . . a delectable escape."
—Darque Reviews on *Kiss of a Dark Moon*

"The interplay between these protagonists sets sparks off the page . . . dark, deadly, and sexy certainly sums up this hero."
—Romantic Times on *Kiss of a Dark Moon*

"Adventurous, witty, and fabulously sexy— definitely a must-read."
—Fresh Fiction on *Marked by Moonlight*

The Moon Chasers novels are also all
available as eBooks.

ALSO BY SHARIE KOHLER

My Soul to Keep
To Crave a Blood Moon
Kiss of a Dark Moon
Marked by Moonlight

Haunted by Your Touch
(with Jeaniene Frost and Shayla Black)

SHARIE KOHLER

NIGHT FALLS ON THE WICKED

THE MOON CHASERS SERIES

POCKET BOOKS

NEW YORK   LONDON   TORONTO   SYDNEY   NEW DELHI

Pocket Books
A Division of Simon & Schuster, Inc.
1230 Avenue of the Americas
New York, NY 10020

First Pocket Books paperback edition September 2011

POCKET and colophon are registered trademarks of Simon & Schuster, Inc.

For information about special discounts for bulk purchases, please contact Simon & Schuster Special Sales at 1-866-506-1949 or business@simonandschuster.com.

The Simon & Schuster Speakers Bureau can bring authors to your live event. For more information or to book an event contact the Simon & Schuster Speakers Bureau at 1-866-248-3049 or visit our website at www.simonspeakers.com.

Interior design by Jacquelynne Hudson
Cover design by Min Choi
Cover art by Craig White

Manufactured in the United States of America

10 9 8 7 6 5 4 3 2 1

ISBN 978-1-4516-1141-0
ISBN 978-1-4516-1143-4 (ebook)

To Lark
reader, writer, cheerleader, a woman
of enviable style and grace.

And above all, friend.

*. . . I found myself within a dark wood,
for the clear path had been lost.*

—DANTE

PROLOGUE

She stood in shadows at the foot of the bed, staring down at the sleeping figure. At sixteen, he was almost a man, but still a boy in so many ways. Always her boy, her son, her baby. A lump thickened her throat and she fought to swallow it down.

He slept fitfully, tossing and turning, sweat glistening on his face, visible even in the room's dull glow. The source of that glow could be seen through the window. It repelled her . . . made her slightly ill. She moved toward the window, her steps creaking over the wooden floor. She grasped the curtains in both hands and pulled the fabric tightly shut as if she could block out that waxing moon. Hide it from view. Forget what it meant, the power it now held over her son.

Her hands lingered on the soft cotton, caressing the fabric for a moment until sliding away. She remembered selecting the curtains years ago. The puppies chasing red balls still made her smile. Of course, *he* had been complaining about them for some time now, arguing that a boy his age needed more manly curtains. Her response had been to laugh, ruffle his hair and tell him he would always be her baby. Nothing would ever change that. Her hands curled into fists, her nails cutting into her tender palms. *Nothing*. Now more than ever she had to be a good mother to him.

It had been just the two of them for so long now. His father was gone. He'd passed in and out of her life so swiftly that memories of him were dim. A man with a rumbling laugh, wicked smile and broad hands that she could hold and stroke and stare at for hours. Niklas remembered nothing of him at all, which was just as well. She'd worked hard over the years to make sure he never felt the lack of a father in his life.

Niklas was her world. And she was his. The realization created a deep gnawing pang in her chest. It was going to be hard for him, but he was young. He'd overcome. He'd grow into a strong man and move on. He'd be fine without her.

She rounded the bed. Her hand shook as she lowered it to his head and brushed the silken hair—almost as though she had never touched him before. Except she had done so every day for the last sixteen years. As her fingers slid the hair back from his feverish skin, she confronted the harsh reality that this would be her last time to touch him. A sob caught in her throat but she held it back, determined not to wake him. Determined that he not know what she was about until it was too late. Until it was done.

Bending, she pressed trembling lips to his cheek. The white bandage peeked out from the edge of his shirt, a painful reminder. Beneath that bandage lay torn flesh that she'd cleaned and cared for the best she could. Not that her efforts made any difference. Raw and ravaged tonight, it would probably be gone tomorrow, miraculously healed. All evidence of his attack would be gone.

She stroked his cheek, trying to memorize the texture, everything about him—enough to make it last. His skin still felt smooth and soft as always, even dangerously warm as he was. The fever was the curse, working its way through him, killing him off bit by bit until only a ghost of him would remain. She wouldn't have that. No matter the cost. It would not come to be.

"Be safe, my love."

And he would, she vowed as she moved from the bed and slipped silently from the room. No matter the price to herself. She'd do what needed to be done. Her son would wake in the morning himself again. Whole and safe.

She, however, would wake far, far from here. And she'd wake as something else. Something without a chance . . . without any hope.

ONE

A gust of late winter wind blew through the open door as another group of loggers tromped inside Sam's Diner. Darby sucked in a breath and tensed against the bitter cold, breathing again when the door thudded shut. Air that cold was something she would never grow accustomed to—even after three years of living in subarctic temperatures.

As the door chimed shut, she hurried with menus to the table—the same as any other night. Handing out menus, refilling glasses, hefting trays of burgers and fries as snow continued to fall in sheets of white outside.

"Darby, girl," a logger with raw, wind-chapped cheeks called to her good-naturedly. "When you gonna marry me?"

Darby pasted a smile on her face and gestured widely with a hand that clutched a coffeepot. "And leave all this?"

The logger snorted. "Who said anything about

leaving this? I was hoping you'd support me. Always wanted to be a kept man."

Darby rolled her eyes. "I'm not keeping anyone on the tips you guys leave me."

His friends laughed. They were good men. Big, burly men who worked hard for a living. She knew many of their names, but nothing else about them. Just as they knew nothing of her. And they never would. She never let anyone close. It wasn't safe to forge relationships.

"Why don't you cut out early? You been here since five," Maggie offered when Darby returned to the counter with their orders.

Darby scanned the narrow diner. At least five tables sat at full occupancy. "Trying to make off with all my tips?" she teased.

Maggie scoffed. They both knew that no one in this town was a big tipper. Not when the majority of residents could barely afford their heating bills.

Maggie waved a thick hand. "You go on. We don't need three waitresses for this crowd." She nodded to Corey at the other end of the diner. "Besides, the kids are at their dad's. Might as well work late. Hate coming home to an empty place."

Darby's smile slipped as she refilled a salt shaker and screwed the lid back on. She knew all about coming home to an empty place. It's all she knew.

"Well, all right then. If you're sure. I don't mind

clocking out early." She nodded to a just-vacated table. "I'll just bus up that one and head out."

"Invitation for dinner tomorrow is still open. Do you good to do something on our day off besides sit around staring at the walls. And my nephew will be there—"

"The taxidermist?"

"Yep. Nicest guy you'll—"

Darby winced. Maggie always knew a nice guy. "No, thanks."

"What?" She sighed, scratching her head with a pencil. "Some reality show marathon on TV?"

An old Alfred Hitchcock movie actually. She always loved the classics—had watched them a lot as a girl with her aunts. Rather than admit this, she shrugged. "Just thought I'd relax, read a book, get in a run—"

"Ugh. Who runs for fun?"

"Lots of people do. It's good exercise." And it helped. Helped keep her mind off things. Gave her a release.

Maggie snorted. "If you had a man you'd be getting plenty of exercise." She laughed at her crude joke.

Darby rolled her eyes. "Trust me, Maggie. You don't want to set your nephew up with me."

Maggie sniffed and swiped at her nose. "Why not?" She leaned close and dropped her voice, her eyes wide, hungry as a hound on the scent. "You hiding from the law or something? That would explain a lot about you, you know."

Darby smiled. Yes. She supposed that would explain a lot, and it would be more plausible than the truth. "No. Nothing like that." She was running from something far worse than the law.

"Well, a date wouldn't hurt. Even Corey's got a date this week." Maggie jerked a thumb to the other waitress.

Corey had a date? The single mom was about as uninterested in dating as Darby was. Well, uninterested wasn't an accurate description exactly. Darby was *interested*. Achingly interested. Some nights she couldn't sleep for all of her *aching* interest. Darby was simply *unable* to date. Big difference.

She watched Corey as she bused a table, her ponytail bouncing as she worked. For some reason the notion of Corey dating made her lonelier than ever. Now Maggie had no one to nag but Darby.

Corey must have seen something on her face. As she passed with a heavily laden tray of drinks, she shook her head at Darby. "Don't let her start on you, Darby. It's just a date. Don't make a big deal out of it, Maggie."

"It *is* a big deal," Maggie flung back. "What's it been for you, Corey? Three years?"

Darby stiffened. Three years. The same amount of time had passed since she'd felt free to go on a date. Since she left home, her family and friends. Three years that yawned on like forever. She swallowed against the sudden tightness in her throat. God—what was the rest of her life going to be like?

She shook her head. It was better than the alternative. She knew that. Was okay with that. Really.

It wasn't an issue of wanting or deserving love. She wanted love, romance. A family, children of her own. She deserved it as much as the next person, but it was never going to happen. It was a beautiful dream. A fantasy.

Reality, sadly, didn't offer any of those things for her. She contented herself with the past—with what little romance she'd had then. Bradley, her off-again, on-again boyfriend through high school. He'd been a good kisser. Had bought her a lovely watch she still owned. And there had been the occasional dates in college. That was all she would ever have.

"Good for Corey," she murmured, fighting back the acrid taste of jealously rising up in her throat. To go out on an actual date. To feel a man's hand on the small of her back as they walked through a crowded room. Darby couldn't deny missing that. Among other things.

Maggie tossed her hands up in the air. "I give up."

Darby grabbed a tub and moved to the table—the familiar need for distance surging back inside her again—and started collecting dishes. She worked quickly, ready to get off her feet and curl up on her couch. The solitude of her cozy room above the diner beckoned. Better that than this—surrounding herself with people that she had to forever and always keep at arm's length. For her sake. For theirs.

She walked back to the kitchen and deposited the heavy tub of dishes next to Sam with a grunt.

"Headed out?" her boss asked around a mouthful of chew, maneuvering the hose in the sink and sending warm water splashing everywhere. Behind him food cooked on the grill, burgers that looked like they needed flipping.

She nodded, slipping off her work shoes and squeezing her feet into her snow boots waiting at the back door. "Yep. Good night."

Sam muttered a response as she slipped on her parka and worked with the double zipper, preparing to leave out the back. "See you Wednesday."

At the sudden thought of her day off tomorrow, she stopped and looked back at her boss. "Hey, Sam, you mind if I come over tomorrow to use your computer for a little bit? I need to look up some stuff."

"Sure. Whenever you need to. We'll be home all day." Of course, he would. Tuesday was the only day of the week the diner was closed and Sam usually spent it relaxing at home with his family.

"Thanks." It was time she started investigating her next move. Maggie's prodding and nosy ways had clued her in that something was off with Darby. It wouldn't take long for others to start wondering about her, too, and the last thing Darby needed was people prying into her life.

Spring was coming. She needed to start planning her next move anyway. She couldn't stay here forever. It was already getting too comfortable. The people here were too nice. Which is why she couldn't stay and put them in jeopardy.

"I'll come over in the afternoon."

"Might as well stay for dinner," he suggested. "Vera's going to make a pot roast."

Darby gave a single nod, not bothering to decline. She wouldn't be staying for dinner. Even as much as she would like to, as much as she craved the company—craved being around a family again. It wasn't to be. It couldn't be.

She knew everyone thought she was odd, antisocial even. And that was fine. Better that than the truth.

Better that than dead.

She shook her head as she stepped outside. The

cold hit her like a fist. She burrowed into her hood and wrapped her scarf around her throat several times, tugging the fabric up to her chin.

Dead. If it was only just that simple. Sadly, there were things worse than death. Her chest tightened. She knew firsthand about such things.

DARBY FINISHED JOTTING DOWN the last of her notes in her spiral, everything she needed to know about Lancaster, Alaska. Population seventeen hundred. A new town for her. One of the only habitable places in Alaska's Arctic Circle. But it needed to be cold during the summer. As far as she was concerned, Lancaster would fit her needs perfectly.

She never visited the same place twice. It was too easy to make friends, to build a life with people in it . . . people who could care about her. She'd discovered that people who cared about her weren't easy to lie to. And lying was all she could do. Unfortunately, the truth wasn't something she could give to anyone. Nor could she give any part of herself. Ever.

She was no good. Tainted. It was in everyone's best interest for her to keep to herself. It was a full-time job to do just that. She missed people, longed for company, a simple friend. It was difficult to stay on guard 24/7, but that's what she had to do.

As long as she lived, that's what she *would* do.

Either that or throw in the towel like her mother did, and Darby couldn't do that. She shivered at the idea. She wasn't a quitter. She'd keep on moving, running, hiding—and try to take what pleasures she could from life in the process.

That was the only thing she could do. The only plan she had. The alternative to that . . .

A chill skated down her spine as she recalled the alternative awaiting her. There was no alternative.

She logged off the computer and gathered her bag, stuffing her spiral inside. She needed to go to the store, but she also wanted to squeeze in a run before it became too dark. The endorphins always helped. Always made everything brighter . . . less depressing now that her life had become this *nonlife*. Not to mention she slept like the dead after a hard run. A deep, dreamless sleep. That was seriously important for her.

Her boots thudded along the wood floor as she left Sam's office and followed the delicious aroma of food into the kitchen.

Vera was setting four plates at the table. Rory, their fourteen-year-old son, sat at the table working on his homework.

She forced a smile.

"Hey, Darby," Rory said, looking up shyly from beneath his shaggy bangs.

"Hey, Rory." She bit back her inclination to ask him what he was studying. She didn't need to know. Didn't need to reveal that she might care.

Darby's gaze moved to the fourth place set at the table, her stomach sinking. Unless they were expecting company, Vera set that plate for her. And she was going to appear rude when she declined. But she had to. Because no way could she stay.

"Find what you were looking for?" Vera inquired.

"Yes. Thanks."

"Well, wash up." She nodded toward the sink. "Supper's almost ready."

"Oh, thanks, but I can't stay."

Vera gave Darby a disapproving glare. "Have plans, do you?"

"Um, yeah."

"Really?" Vera arched a brow as she wiped her hands on a checked dishcloth. "Because you sure haven't done much around this town since you moved here, not counting jogging and working long hours for Sam. Such a shame . . . a pretty girl like you should—"

"Thanks for letting me use your computer, Vera," Darby cut in, unwilling to suffer the well-meaning lecture when she could offer no explanation as to why a young woman would prefer to live a life of isolation.

Vera released a defeated sigh. "Sure, any time." She slapped the dish towel over her shoulder and shook her head as if Darby was a creature beyond her understanding.

Once on the porch, Darby met Sam coming in with an armful of wood for the fireplace. Warm air puffed in a cloud from his lips. He frowned at her. "Let me guess. You're not staying for dinner."

"No." She shook her head. "Thanks though."

"Well, let me walk you into town."

"That's not necessary," she protested.

He frowned. "With the wolves acting up lately, it is necessary."

"Sam, it's a short walk into town." She motioned down the driveway to the squat buildings outlined in the near distance. "And it's still daylight. None of the attacks have happened during the day. I'll be fine."

He scratched his bristly jaw, looking uncertain.

"Stop worrying, Sam. Go eat your dinner and enjoy the rest of your day off." Her boots thudded down the wooden steps of his porch. She was halfway down his drive when she looked back over her shoulder to see Sam still standing there, watching her. "See! I'm halfway to town and no problems!"

He waved a hand after her, but she could see his lips twitch. It warmed her heart—as it shouldn't—to make him smile.

She had always been able to make her aunts smile. She hardly remembered those days with them anymore. It had been a long time since she'd made anyone smile or laugh. You had to be close to someone for that to happen.

She tromped down the well-traveled road, following in the tire tracks, where the snow was the smoothest and flattest and it took less work to walk. The pines on either side of her thinned out as she entered the town, passing first the post office and the squat, square building that was the city courthouse.

A couple descended the courthouse steps, their hands laced together. They walked close, leaning into each other. The woman dropped her head against his shoulder as if she couldn't resist, as if she had to touch him, had to be close. He turned and pressed a tender kiss to her cheek. She smiled and stretched her hand out in front of her, wriggling her fingers, admiring the modest wedding ring, and Darby guessed they'd just tied the knot in the courthouse.

Something tightened in her chest, a familiar pang at the sight of what she could never have, what could never be hers. *Damn it. She was maudlin lately.*

She turned her gaze away and increased her pace, avoiding the sight of them as if that would shield her from the sad state of her own life and what it was always destined to be. Her mother had known what awaited her, had whispered it in her ear as she brushed her hair every night at bedtime.

There are worse things than being alone, Darby. Never forget that. Mommy won't be here for you forever. Someday you'll be alone. If you're smart, you'll learn to accept it. Don't be weak and stupid like me and let a man sweet-talk his way into your life. The last thing you need is a baby.

Hard stuff for an eight-year-old to hear at bedtime. Only she hadn't realized it. At age eight, it didn't occur to her to be insulted. She'd simply nodded and agreed. *Yes, Mommy.*

She didn't understand then what she knew now—that her mother regretted her father . . . that she regretted Darby. Now that she knew that, now that she was alone just as her mother had predicted, it was her mother's voice she constantly heard in her head. That voice kept her strong, kept her on track.

Always remember, Darby, that there are real-life monsters out there, ready to gobble you up, possess you, turn you into the same horrible monsters they are. Just like your aunt Lena.

Aunt Lena made nationwide news when she burned down her office building, killing three and injuring several more. She'd disappeared before she could be apprehended. Law enforcement assumed she'd headed for Mexico, but Darby's family knew she was headed for cooler climes. Someplace where she could wrest some control from the demon possessing her, the entity that was pure evil and forcing her to do terrible things. Like burn down buildings. And kill.

As soon as it started to get bad for Darby, once the demons came for her almost nightly, plaguing her constantly, she took her mother's advice.

Better sooner than later. She wasn't going to wait until a demon possessed her and forced her to kill somebody. Three years ago the demons had become particularly bothersome, invading her dreams, terrorizing her at every turn.

Just as they had done with her mother.

So as her mother recommended, Darby chose the path that didn't just keep her safe, it kept the world safe.

It was as simple as that.

Across the street, Maggie stepped out of the hardware store. She waved widely and called out. Darby stared straight ahead, deliberately avoiding her, snuggling deeper into her parka, sealing herself inside herself.

And sealing the world out.

TWO

Niklas pulled up in front of the small B&B, the only lodging available in the small town where he'd tracked his prey.

He grimaced at the two-story, whitewashed house with its picket fence. In bigger cities he had the benefit of anonymity. By the end of the night everyone would know about the lone man in their midst. There would be stares, prying questions—none of which he would answer. Even if he did, no one would believe him.

At least the house sat directly on Main Street, where he could see most everything going on in the town. With this heartening thought, he stepped out of the vehicle and sucked in a bracing breath at the sudden cold, unexpected even though he'd been chasing his quarry through Canada for the last two months now.

The air cut into him and he shivered and burrowed deeper into his coat and wondered why the bastards had to pick the Great White North as their newest area to terrorize. He inhaled deeply, sniffing the air, searching for any lingering scent of them, hoping they were still here. His skin prickled and tightened in that familiar way that told him they were here. Close.

He stared down the two-lane street. A truck approached, driving slowly through the curling white air that seemed to float everywhere. A big, thick-furred dog hopped around the back, jumping madly on his paws. His shiny dark eyes rolled wildly as he barked fiercely at Niklas. The driver yelled back for him to shut up, but the dog couldn't silence himself.

Niklas stared impassively as the truck drove by, bearing the dog away. The dog knew. Sensed what Niklas was. Or rather what he wasn't.

Opening the back door, he grabbed his gear from the back—three black duffel bags. Everything he would need to continue his hunt. Infrared goggles, winter camo, guns, knives, vials of silver nitrate, maps of the surrounding area. If it could be of use, he had it.

After checking in and avoiding the nosy clerk's questions, he grabbed the local newspaper on the counter before tromping up the narrow stairs to his room.

He passed a maid carrying towels on the stairs. She moved to the side for him to pass, her wide eyes devouring him. He was instantly aware of her increased heart rate and the spike in her body temperature.

"Hi," she said, her voice breathy. Her gaze slid over his tall form, licked him up and down like she'd never seen a tastier treat.

He nodded once in greeting.

As he brushed past her, he felt her body tremor with excitement. She pushed up off the wall. "I'm Holly," she blurted after him. "If you need anything, just call down to the front and ask for me."

Her need filled his nostrils, a heady thing that could overtake him if he let it. Fortunately, he'd mastered control, well aware that it wasn't actually him, not the *real* him that drew her. Sure, he was better than average, he guessed, but looks alone couldn't get him laid within five seconds flat of meeting a woman. It was something more. She was responding to that part of him that he loathed. The magnetism that belonged to the beast.

Years of living this way—simply being what he was—had taught him to cope with moments like this. Even though instinct urged him to take her, seize her and what she offered him like a rutting beast, he was able to ignore the hunger as it flared to life, recognizing it for the meaningless desire it was.

The beast within him was all about primal

urges. Fucking was a part of that. He didn't resist it all the time. Sometimes he answered the call, but he wasn't like the others, his brethren, insatiable beasts that never resisted an urge. Not to fuck. Not to kill and feed.

He opened the door to his room, not bothering to look back and see if the maid still stood there. He could feel her. He knew she watched him.

Shutting the door behind him, he dropped his gear and moved to the room's sole window. He'd requested a view of the street. If they were out there, stalking the town's residents, it increased his odds of spotting them.

He looked down at the newspaper still clutched in his hand. The headline stood out boldly in black, block letters: *Wolf Threat Still Unresolved!*

He snorted.

And it likely wouldn't be resolved. Not unless he resolved it. Or they gave him the slip and moved on to new hunting grounds. Again.

He curled the newspaper in his hand until it crumpled. Not again. He wouldn't lose them again. This was it. He finally had them. Cyprian would be his.

Across the street a figure walked, bent slightly forward as though fighting the wind. Despite the bulky jacket, he marked her as female. His gaze moved away from her, scanning up and down the street, but then his gaze drifted back to her again. Something drew his eye. She wasn't what he hunted, so he wasn't sure what it was about her that snared his attention.

He could make nothing of her face set within the dark blue hood of her parka, but his skin tightened as he followed her progress down the sidewalk.

He studied her closely, eyeing the slim length of her legs in her fitted black pants. They were nice. Long and shapely. It was probably just that. He needed a woman. He thought back, trying to recall the last time he'd had sex. Maybe he should call down for Holly after all.

He moved from the window and went back to his bags, organizing his gear with new determination for the night's hunt. He couldn't distract himself this close to his goal—this close to capturing the lycan who'd infected him and robbed him of his mother, damning her soul and sentencing him to an empty life, forever trapped between two worlds. Forever alone.

THREE

After work the following day, Darby regretted not squeezing in her much-needed trip to the grocery store on her day off. She glanced at her watch as she left the diner. The store closed in another half hour. Barely enough time, but she was low on milk. Since she didn't particularly enjoy dry cereal, she figured she'd just have to postpone her run. This wasn't a big city where the store kept late hours. Family-owned, it pretty much shut down right at eight.

Halfway down the block from the diner, she hesitated for a moment. A crowd was gathered at the end of the street in front of the grocery store. She didn't do crowds. Not if she could help it. She never knew what might trigger a vision, but she knew that more people around her seemed to increase the odds.

Hovering there, she stomped her boots on the sidewalk, shaking snow loose, trying to pretend there was a reason for her standing in the middle of the sidewalk as she tried to make up her mind about whether to brave the crowd or not.

Things had been smooth lately, better than expected actually. Isolating herself, keeping a low profile was working apparently. She hadn't suffered a vision in over a year, but that didn't mean she was free. She'd never be free. She could never return home and she wouldn't be so naïve as to think that she could.

Staring down the crowd with narrowed eyes, she clenched her jaw and strode forward with hard steps. She'd given up enough already. She wasn't going to go hungry—even for one night. Nor was she going to go back to the diner and eat one of Sam's greasy burgers either. One for lunch had been enough. Tonight she planned on enjoying a little pasta with basil and a glass of wine. She sighed in pleasure, almost as though she could taste it now.

Besides, it wasn't like she was going to hang around and rub elbows with the lot of them. She'd be in and out in a flash. She'd walk directly past the crowd into the store, buy what she needed and be gone. With a decisive nod, she stepped forward.

As she neared the store, she saw everyone grouped around a beat-up old pickup truck, peering inside the back. A man stood in the truck bed wearing full camouflage.

"No thanks needed!" he called out with a wide wave to the crowd. "Every once in a while someone needs to show the wild beasts of the world that we're masters of this land!"

The nape of her neck tingled in warning as he bent down with a grunt, and she knew something was coming that she wasn't going to like. She told herself to turn, to walk away and not look, not watch what was unfolding, but her feet were rooted to the earth.

She gasped when he came back up with a grunt, hefting the carcass of a wolf. He showed off his trophy with pride to the crowd. Blood stained the brown and gray fur. The animal's dead eyes stared out lifelessly—like inanimate marbles.

Clapping and hoots of approval erupted from the crowd. Darby looked away, unwilling to stare too long into the creature's frozen eyes. She'd seen enough in that one glimpse. It was there, locked in the wolf's expression, that last moment of life when he realized it was all over. She read the fear, the panic still mirrored there that begged for more time—for life.

More cheering exploded. She risked another glance only to see a second wolf hoisted for display.

She almost imagined she could feel the tattoo on her shoulder tingling with a kindred connection . . . an awareness of sorts. Crazy, she knew. She'd gotten the tat a few years ago, after leaving Seattle, leaving her aunts and cousins—after she'd said good-bye to Jonah.

Jonah. She sighed at the memory of him. He'd been her friend—a demon slayer made a particularly *good* friend to have. She hadn't thought of him in a while. She missed him—hoped he was happy with Sorcha. It took Darby only a glimpse of them together to see that Jonah would never be hers . . . that her feelings for him would never be returned. They would only ever be friends.

He'd taught her a valuable lesson though—that not everything was what it appeared to be. It was a lesson she never forgot. Jonah should have been something feared and reviled, something as evil as the very *things* that hunted her. Instead, he'd been her savior on more than one occasion. Before she took on a life of isolation and had to start looking out for herself.

The tattoo of the wolf that covered her left shoulder blade served as a reminder of everything Jonah had taught her . . . and of the past she'd left behind. It gave her some connection to everything and everyone she'd lost. It made her feel less alone.

She bypassed the crowd and made her way quickly through the store, grabbing some milk, a fresh loaf of bread and some basil. Even walking through the aisles, she could still hear the furor outside.

The cashier, too busy staring raptly out the storefront window, hardly looked at Darby as she paid. With the recent attacks, those dead wolves were more than a pair of trophies. They symbolized justice to the townspeople. Darby shook her head, sad at just how wrong they were—and at how the innocent animals had to suffer for their mistake.

With her small bag in her arms, she sucked in a breath before emerging outside again—almost as if she were about to dive into a dense fog of poison. Anyone watching would have assumed she was bracing herself for the cold and not the mob overflowing the parking lot.

She couldn't help eyeing the scene as she walked, fiddling with her scarf at her neck to better cover her chin and mouth, not watching where she was going and running smack into the back of someone.

It was like hitting a wall. She fell backward, her bag of groceries falling onto the ground. Elbows in the snow, she watched as a small tub of butter rolled several feet away before stopping.

Embarrassed, she hopped up and quickly began gathering her things, her boots crunching over the snow-buried ground. She didn't look up. Not even when the man she'd run into squatted beside her and handed her the loaf of bread. She kept her eyes averted, muttering beneath her breath.

This was something she'd mastered. Never looking at people directly. When you looked them in the face, people talked to you way too long and tried to dig past the exterior. *Never engage.* She lived by this mantra. That's why waitressing worked so well for her—even if the pay was barely enough to keep her clothed and fed. No one really wanted to talk to their server. People just wanted their food and to be left alone. A waitress was practically invisible—and invisible was what she'd set out to become.

Accepting the bread from the stranger, her gaze locked on his hand. All of her stilled at the sight. Even her lungs ceased to draw breath.

His hand was masculine, the wrist strong and narrow. Capable. The back of it lightly sprinkled with fair hairs and traced with faint veins. The sight was all achingly familiar. Although not in a specific way. It wasn't a specific hand belonging to a specific man.

Her reaction was familiar. Her single-minded focus something she'd felt before. Back when she didn't want to be invisible. When she yearned for Jonah to notice her.

She remembered what it felt like to center all

her attention on a single masculine hand, hoping she would look up and find *his* eyes on her, seeing her. Finally, truly, seeing her. At last.

She recalled how her chest would tighten at the glimpse of his hand, the brush of tapering fingers against any part of her. She'd spend hours lost in daydreams of what it would feel like to have that hand touch her, stroke her until she arched and purred like a cat beneath his expert ministrations.

Despite the bitter cold, she suddenly felt hot, flushed with warmth. This hand sparked something deep inside her, woke a dormant piece of herself she'd only ever felt stir and come alive around Jonah. Useless as her feelings had been. Jonah had never looked at her that way, never felt that kind of attraction for her. And now his heart belonged to another.

She snatched up her bread with a muttered thanks, grateful the girl she used to be was gone. She wasn't the same girl of three years ago, given to girlish infatuations. She didn't become giddy and experience butterflies for a guy with nice hands. She wasn't the type to languish after a guy. She wasn't even the type to waste her breath talking to one anymore. There wasn't any point after all.

"Sorry." Stuffing the rest of her things back into the sack, she rose to her feet. "I wasn't looking where I was going." She let herself look at him then, having regained control of herself.

And then she lost it again. Her composure flew away.

It was like coming face-to-face with an angel. Dropped from sky to earth, he stood right in front of her.

Her mouth sagged a little as she drank him in—the deeply set indigo eyes, the square jaw and perfectly carved lips. Fascinating creases carved into each cheek just alongside his lips. Lips made for kissing. She swallowed past the sudden thickness in her throat.

"It's okay," he murmured in a distracted manner, looking more at the crowd than her . . . which was a relief but also a blow to her ego. "Quite a show going on, huh?"

If his face didn't push her over the edge into infatuation, then the voice did. The sound of it stroked her like satin on naked flesh. There was an accent there. She had no idea of the origins. Faintly crisp and rolling. British maybe? Her toes curled inside her boots.

She gave herself a mental shake to snap out of her stupor. She'd been fine these last few years without a man in her life. She didn't need one now.

She didn't *want* to need one now.

She looked with longing across the street to the sidewalk that would carry her home. Home to safety and solitude. The two were dependent upon each other.

"It's a circus all right," she returned, recovering her voice, the well-worn indifference. She shifted her weight on her feet, anxious to be on her way.

He looked at her then, truly looked at her, and she wondered why she'd said anything at all. Why didn't she just take her bag and go, flee, instead of lingering here?

What was she hoping for? God, was she even *hoping*? When she'd given up on hope years ago?

"Yeah," he returned, looking her over with slow appraisal. Those impossible indigo eyes of his altered, became something . . . unnatural.

She struggled not to fidget beneath their regard. It seemed that they almost glowed, lit from within. She shook her head, convinced she was going crazy. Just desperate and lonely enough that her imagination was running wild.

"A real circus," he said, echoing her.

Something shivered its way inside her at his drawling voice that said nothing remarkable and yet did.

Even as she told herself to break away—walk, run even—she couldn't budge her feet. His eyes spoke to her, told her to stay put. It was almost as if he mesmerized her . . . trapped her in a spell.

When he glanced back to the milling people, a breath escaped her that she hadn't realized she'd been holding. With those eyes off her now, she felt more in control of herself.

"They're definitely not a fan of wolves around here, huh?" he asked.

"You could say that," she hedged. "They don't have the most open minds around here. Just be glad you're not a wolf," she joked, but something came over him, a sudden tensing of his broad shoulders that she didn't miss.

He looked back at her again, expectantly, as if he waited for her to continue, to say more.

"There's been a few alleged wolf attacks," she elaborated, compelled to fill the awkward silence. "Lately everyone's armed to the teeth around here."

"Ah." He nodded in the direction of the truck. Hair that was a myriad colors, several shades of gold and brown, fell across his brow. Somewhere, not in towns like this, women spent thousands of dollars in a salon to get hair like that. Something told her this guy didn't do a thing except shampoo. He was effortlessly gorgeous. And her throat felt suddenly tight and dry with this realization. "Then those are the fearsome animals responsible for the alleged attacks?"

"Those two?" She snorted against the bite of cold air and pulled the hood of her coat closer around her face, swiping at her red-tipped nose. "Unlikely. Those wolves hardly look like they've eaten all winter. I don't think they've attacked anyone. But no one's convincing the local rabble otherwise."

His well-carved lips twitched and she thought he wanted to smile, but then the hint of curving lips was gone, replaced with the stoic mask again.

It was as though he forgot her presence. His gaze traveled over the locals, assessing, almost as if he were looking for someone, marking each and every one of them.

With his attention removed from her, she finally turned and hurried away, her steps crunching quickly over the snow-covered sidewalk. She felt like a criminal on the escape. Silly, she knew. She didn't even know his name. Good-byes weren't a requirement. He was just a stranger. That's all he could ever be. All she could let him be despite her instant attraction to him. Despite how much she still wanted to linger and talk to him.

She watched her breath fog before her lips and tried to forget those eyes—that stare. Easier said than done. She hadn't found herself in close conversation with a good-looking guy in forever.

She was better off not getting involved. With him. With anyone.

He was better off. Everyone was.

And yet several feet down the street, she could not resist another look back. Just to assess. Just to make sure he wasn't looking after her. He wasn't. And for that, she felt a stab of disappointment that she had no business feeling.

FOUR

When Niklas looked back, she was gone.

He quickly scanned the small parking lot and spotted her ahead, continuing down the sidewalk with her bag of groceries and her blue hood pulled low over her head, obscuring her profile. He suspected this wasn't just because of the cold but because she didn't like to draw attention to herself. She had a way about her—a quiet way of moving, almost as though she didn't touch the ground when she walked. Of course he noticed her. He missed nothing or no one.

He'd known instantly it was her. The woman he'd seen walking across the street from the B&B yesterday. Aside from his recognizing the coat she wore, his body had reacted instantly, his skin jumping and tightening the same way it had yesterday.

He felt a stab of disappointment to see her go. A strange sensation. He had barely viewed her face and he hadn't even glimpsed her hair. Just a vague impression of a pale face and wide hazel eyes. Nothing remarkable—on the surface. But there was something more there, something lurking beneath. Something that caught his attention. Yesterday and now. Something that held his *rarely* caught attention.

He frowned at her brisk pace. She was practically jogging. It was almost as if she were fleeing. From him? Had he frightened her? Those hazel eyes had stared at him with a wide-eyed awareness. At first, he thought she recognized him. Impossible, he knew. He knew no one. Had no one. He was all alone in this world and had been for too many years to count.

He considered following her. She wouldn't live far if she was on foot in this climate. He took one step in the direction she'd fled and then stopped himself. Shaking his head, he wondered why he should care where she lived. But he knew that answer deep and swift in his blood. Just as he knew himself.

He hadn't spent this long keeping himself tightly in check without coming to understand precisely what he was.

She turned a corner in front of the town diner. Out of sight. His breath came easier. He'd felt a connection to her. A response. It was all tied up in his baser instincts. No matter how he struggled to suppress his nature, the essence of what he was rose up inside him now and then. A bitter reminder just in case he started to feel normal. In case he started believing he was an average guy.

There was no formula as to what female might arouse a reaction in him. No predicting. Yesterday, the maid, Holly, had been easy enough to pass by, to reject. But this one . . .

He shook his head, the satin-soft sound of her voice still running through his mind

Certain women affected him more than others. Every once in a while he got within breathing distance of a specific female and a primal need seized him to take her, have her, possess her. She was one of them, he guessed. Nothing more.

Usually he walked away as fast as he could manage when one of those situations occurred. A few times, admittedly, he didn't walk away.

A few times he succumbed. Sometimes when he was feeling particularly weak he took what he craved, what the woman invited, and then he left. As quickly as possible.

Tonight, she was gone before he had a chance to decide for himself if he wanted to pursue her. A heavy sigh welled up inside him and pushed past his lips. Just as well.

He returned his attention to the idiots cheering over a few wolf corpses. It was the same story everywhere. Sad, really, that wolves got blamed for the attacks.

Alleged. That was the word the girl had used. He hadn't missed that. She was smart. He'd heard it in her voice, watched it in the movement of her body. She held herself guardedly, with a certain awareness. She *knew* that wolves weren't behind the attacks. Although, he knew, she couldn't fathom the true reason. Who would? But for him, the conclusion was obvious.

The killings had occurred in the last moonrise. He only hoped it was the pack he was after. He'd lost track of them in Calgary, but from the moment he arrived here he knew they were close. He felt them, scented their presence. He slid a glance up at the night sky. The waxing moon burned through the clouds, almost full. There wasn't much time. Just a few more days. With any luck, he'd find them before moonrise.

Before someone else died.

AS SOON AS DARBY got home she hurriedly put away her groceries and changed into her running clothes. As exhausting as work could be, running brought her back to life. She figured it was the endorphin release. She read somewhere that endorphins made you happier. In her case, it probably staved off the despair from consuming her. Not to mention it kept her in shape. Something necessary with the amount of diner food she ate.

For some reason, her run-in with the hot guy in front of the store only made her feel more on edge than normal. She definitely needed to pound out some frustration on the pavement.

She passed the front of the diner, waving to Maggie through the windows. She and Corey had the late shift tonight. Tomorrow would be Darby's turn.

She deliberately didn't look in the direction of the store. She didn't want to know if the stranger was still standing there. She didn't want to look at the hot guy that made her skin ripple, her body ache and long for a man's touch. Nor did she really want to see a bunch of locals cheering over some wolf carcasses.

She pushed on, moving into the quieter section of town. The cold didn't affect her once she got her heart pumping and legs moving. She stayed within the town, working her way from one end to the other.

It was already dark, but the streetlamps lighted her way. She glanced up past the craggy mountain peaks to the moon. Not quite full. It wasn't as if she had that to worry about. *Yet*.

She passed the B&B and noticed a black Hummer parked in front. Immediately, her mind went to the guy from earlier tonight, the stranger, and she just knew it was his. No one around here drove anything like it. Her gaze skimmed the several windows dotting the front of the quaint B&B, wondering which one might be his.

With a shake of her head and a groan, she increased her speed and turned off Main onto one of the older residential streets. It was a street she liked running down because the houses were older. Charming and picturesque with large, wraparound porches. Colorful gardens in the spring and summer. Not that she was ever here to see them then, but she bet they looked beautiful. She liked to imagine them, liked to fantasize about the sun on her face.

The Christmas lights were down now, but they'd been beautiful. It was as if all the neighbors had some sort of unspoken agreement to try to outdo one another. Her aunts used to take great care over Christmas, including decorating the house. Such things had never been priorities for her mother, but for her aunts Christmas was big. They would have arguments over what color lights should go on the outside of the house. A pained smile flitted over her lips. She shook her head and pushed her legs harder, fighting through the burn in her lungs.

Her breath puffed out in front of her as she followed the curving sidewalk, turning with the street as it ended in a cul-de-sac. She backtracked on the opposite side of the street now, the cadence of her thundering feet feeding her spirit.

The world slipped away, fading to nothing save dark night ahead of her, the only sound in her head the sawing of her own breath.

AS NIKLAS NEARED THE front door of the B&B, ready to tackle the night and scour the area for Cyprian and the others, he spotted her through the window. She was across the street, running. Stepping outside, he burrowed into his coat and watched as she moved down the sidewalk at a fast clip.

He shook his head. Who jogged in weather like this? And at night. Alone. *Alone at night.*

He scowled as this occurred to him, sinking in. She was the perfect target for Cyprian and his pack. She probably thought she was safe in town. No way could she predict the danger that lurked.

Even without the full moon it was dangerous. *They* were never harmless. Although he told himself it wasn't his concern—*she* wasn't his concern—he took off after her, moving swiftly, faster than the eye could process. Like the curls of icy air traveling over the frozen streets, he followed her without detection. That was his gift. Or curse.

She jogged through a neighborhood, fast for

a human, bounding effortlessly it seemed. He admired her movements as he kept a safe distance. She wore a jogging jacket, fitted and smooth against her body, designed for winter. Her thumbs poked out of small holes in the sleeves. From her flowing, natural stride he surmised she ran a lot. The neighborhood sat silent, nestled among shadows and trees. His lips twisted and he felt an unreasonable flash of anger. She made an easy target, so easy to claim. Careless fool. Even without blood-hungry creatures wandering the night, the woman should be smarter.

He stilled at the end of the street, leaning against the frozen post that held up the crooked street sign as he waited for her to return.

She almost didn't see him until she was on top of him. She jerked back with a startled yelp, her wide-eyed gaze falling on him. Her hood fell back from her head and he was granted his first view of her hair. Even in a ponytail he could see that it was a dark red, thick as a horse mane in its band.

She hopped a little where she stood, her hot breath blowing clouds in front of her. "I didn't see you there," she panted.

"You should pay attention." He crossed his arms across his chest. "It's called situational awareness."

Her flushed cheeks burned brighter, almost as

bright as the frozen red tip of her nose. "Thanks for the tip. You're right, of course." She looked him up and down. "You never know what dirtbag you can run into."

He had to stop himself from laughing. She wasn't scared of him. Or at least she didn't show it. Nor was she hot to rip off his clothes and get dirty in bed with him. Those were the two reactions he was accustomed to inciting in the opposite sex. Fear and lust. He was mildly disappointed the latter was missing.

Instead of desire, she looked at him with annoyance.

"With the wolf attacks going on, you should reconsider jogging at night," he advised.

"Yeah? Somebody make you the neighborhood watch on your second day in town?"

He smiled. "How do you know it's my second day?"

"Lucky guess."

He dug his fists deeper into his pockets and scanned the silent street. "Anyone else new come to town recently? About a month ago? I'm looking for a few buddies . . ."

Her hazel eyes narrowed on him. "And you lost them? Mustn't be too tight with these buddies of yours."

She was smart. He'd give her that.

"Look." She sighed and reached up to pull her ponytail tighter. "All anyone can talk about is the wolf situation lately. The first attack was around a month ago. If any newcomers arrived around that time, they wouldn't have earned a lot of attention. You want to know anything, ask Dollie at the post office. She knows everything."

"Dollie. I'll keep that in mind."

She gave a brusque nod.

"You really shouldn't jog alone at night," he couldn't resist adding, still bothered at the idea of her putting herself at risk.

"I'll keep that in mind."

With that, she pulled her hood back over her head and continued running. He watched her as she advanced down Main, tempted to follow her again. At least she was beneath the bright streetlamps now. For some reason that mattered to him.

Instead of pursuing her again, he moved toward his car. Playing hero was a wholly new sentiment for him. It was especially pointless when the damsels didn't want rescuing.

He had a mission. The longer he delayed, the more people died. And the longer vengeance went unserved.

FIVE

Darby made it through another day at work without any more encounters with the stranger. She wondered if he'd already left. No one stayed here long after all. You were either born and bred in this town or just passing through. Like her, he wouldn't be sticking around.

She didn't know what to make of him. She guessed he wasn't the murdering rapist variety or he would have finished her off last night. Even though he'd done nothing more than caution her about jogging alone at night—something a nice guy would do—she was convinced he wasn't a *nice* guy. Nice guys didn't look the way he did. They didn't have eyes like his that *glowed*. Eyes that made her decidedly uncomfortable.

She finished her cereal bar and took a swig of juice. Reclining on her couch, she watched the television blindly, her mind drifting, returning to last night and *him*.

She supposed it was natural. She couldn't

remember the last time she'd talked to a hot guy. She felt like a schoolgirl with her first crush. She replayed their conversations over and over in her head, thinking about what he said, what she said . . . what she could have said *better*.

She groaned and shook her head side to side. She didn't know why she was so bothered with any of it. None of it mattered.

She refocused her gaze on the television. Usually true crime shows riveted her. Her feet were propped up on the old chest that served as her coffee table. She wiggled her tired, numb toes. After a long day on her feet, it would be easy to blow off her planned run and veg out. But she could veg later. More important, she never slept quite as well as she did after a run. She slept like the dead—a deep, dreamless sleep. The kind of sleep no demon could invade. And wasn't that the point? The point of everything? Her whole life.

Running from demons.

With a deep breath, she pushed up from the couch and turned off the TV. Glancing out the blinds, she saw that daylight was fading. She frowned, telling herself she could push it hard for thirty minutes and beat full dark.

And why should that matter? a small voice demanded. An *unwanted* voice because it wasn't hers. It was *his*. His advice had stuck with her, and she couldn't deny he was right. She shouldn't be out alone at night. Especially with people getting killed around town.

Ignoring the voice, she laced up her shoes and left her apartment at a hard run. Her feet beat the pavement quick and fierce. As she passed the B&B, she couldn't stop herself from looking. The Hummer was gone and a sinking sensation filled her. Had he left town for good?

She pushed harder, sprinting now, air fogging from her lips and nose as she turned left off Main, following the sidewalk through a neighborhood of brick houses with smoking chimneys.

She spotted Corey's house ahead. Or rather, Corey's mom's house. Corey and her little boy lived there with her. As her shoes pounded the snow-covered sidewalk, a truck roared past and pulled into Corey's driveway. Even with the window rolled up, heavy rock blared from the inside. The driver laid on the horn once. In moments, Corey was coming out her door and skipping down the front steps of her porch. Darby guessed this was the "date."

Darby ran past their house to the end of the street and turned around. The truck's taillights glowed in the night. Bad manners or not, she felt herself envying Corey her date.

She picked up the pace, her legs working harder,

the air sawing from her mouth faster. She turned back onto Main, intent on exorcising those feelings. Determined to rid herself of every emotion, every feeling except the ache in her muscles and the reliable burn in her lungs.

Her legs stretched long as she passed the various storefronts of downtown, her pumping arms cutting through the dry, cold air. It helped. This helped. She didn't feel sorry for herself when she worked her body hard. She didn't think about anything, not about the friends and family she left behind, not the empty days and nights that lay ahead of her. Not about the stranger from the night before that roused all kinds of longing inside her. It was nothing but this. Her body in perfect, fluid motion.

Almost home now, she was sweating beneath her clothes. The sun had dipped behind the snow-covered mountains and a faint haze of red washed the air. She circled to the back of the diner and pounded up the steps to her apartment. Inside, she paced the small space of her living room, cooling herself down. She grabbed a bottled water from the refrigerator and took a swig.

Her buzz was still there, a euphoria that would last her through the night and ease her into the deep, dreamless sleep she needed. Moving into her bedroom, she stripped off her clothes and turned on the shower, waiting for the water to warm.

Still, just to be safe, she strolled naked back into the living room and flipped on the television and found an old movie, welcoming the noise, the distraction. It filled the silence and made her life seem less . . . *less*.

Anything to keep her thoughts off the cloying quiet, the suffocating aloneness of her life.

Corey slammed the door shut with all her might, swearing when a nail broke in a sharp burst of pain. Hands on her hips, she glared through the dirty truck window at her date.

"Don't call me again," she bit out, and then stomped away, churning the snow with her boots. It was only a couple of miles back to town. She wasn't afraid of walking.

The truck pulled up alongside her, the diesel fumes choking her. She waved a hand to clear the stink.

"Come on, Corey," Don cajoled. "Don't be that way."

"Leave me alone." Why had she ever agreed to go out with him in the first place? She shouldn't have listened to her mother. So what if he had a solid job and his own house? That didn't make suffering through his rough gropings worth it.

"You don't want to walk to town in this cold. C'mon, sweetheart."

"It beats getting back in the cab with you."

"Corey!" Apparently he thought taking an authoritative voice would win her over. "Get in the truck!"

He would be wrong on that score. She could almost feel the steam coming out of her ears. She'd had enough with overbearing men in her life. First her daddy, and then her husband. If Tommy hadn't run off the road after an all-night bender and wrapped himself around a tree, she'd still be stuck with him and his quick fists. With the slaps that made her ears ring. With choking tears and sobs she had to stifle so she didn't wake up Parker.

"Go to hell," she flung at him. She was twenty-seven. She still had a lot of life left. She didn't need a man. She had a decent job and Parker. He was all she needed.

"Fine, bitch! Hope you freeze." He gunned the truck. The tires spit a spray of grimy snow on her, dousing her new pair of jeans. She watched the taillights fade into the night, not the least bit sorry.

With a tired sigh, she continued down the road. The moon rode high above the tall trees, following her as she made her way back to town. Its pale light reflected off the snow. The night floated like a pool of ink around her. Striding ahead, she felt as if she swam through it. The distant lights of town winked at her through the occasional break in the trees.

Her pace increased as she thought of her warm bed, her television, Parker asleep in his bed in the room next to hers. For the first time in her life, she was okay with what she had—with what she was. She didn't need more than that. She didn't need some jerk draggin' her down.

The first howl stopped her cold in her tracks. It was like no wolf's howl she'd ever heard before, and she'd grown up out here, where wolves were part of life. You didn't camp or hike the trails in the summer without glimpsing or hearing an occasional wolf.

Their distant cries, hoarse and hollow-sounding, had always made her a little sad, a part of herself recognizing the loneliness in their calls.

A howl came again and the hairs on the back of her neck stood on end. Terror struck her heart, quick as a deep-slicing blade.

She was running clumsily by the time she heard the third howl. And the fourth. She was panting and sobbing, her boots hitting the hard tire tracks in the road when she realized they were all around her, running along both sides of her, gliding in effortless, loping grace through the dense trees that crowded the road.

Her heart beat like a wild bird in her chest,

desperate to burst free and escape to another place. She caught glimpses of them through the trees, ghostly figures that kept pace with her, that seemed too large to be wolves. *Bears?*

"God, please, please . . ."

She sobbed ugly, raw sounds and lost her balance, falling onto the uneven road. She staggered back to her feet. Their howls filled the air in a terrible cacophony of sound. They toyed with her. They could have had her by now. She was sure of this.

Elation filled her as suddenly lights appeared ahead, dipping and rising with the undulating road. Headlights. Someone was coming. Adrenaline shot through her, mingling with a sudden burst of joy, the wild hope for survival.

She was moving again, her arms pumping hard, her legs faster. She was going to be all right.

"Hey!" she cried, her voice wild in the suddenly silent air. She waved her arms violently over her head.

The night held its breath all around. No more howls. The trees were still. The only sound she heard was the low hum of the distant car approaching and the rush of blood in her overexerted veins.

She slowed to a stop. Bending at the waist, she pressed her hands against her thighs and squinted, peering intently into the press of foliage, into the sparkling snow and ice-covered undergrowth.

Nothing. They were gone. Nothing lurked there except the bite of a late-clinging winter. They must have heard the car coming. She was going to be okay. She released a shuddery laugh, straightening.

Then the trees shifted, something moved, and she realized she wasn't staring at the glint of ice upon trees at all, but a pair of silver eyes.

The thing moved so fast she couldn't process, couldn't absorb. She only knew that it wasn't a wolf coming at her.

And then there was nothing else.

DARBY JERKED FROM SLEEP with a sharp gasp, lurching upright in her bed to the usual sounds of her apartment. The rattling heater fighting to work, the steady click of the wall clock, the creak of the mattress springs as she shifted her weight.

And another sound. An unfamiliar sound. It scraped down her spine and she shivered beneath the heavy bedding.

She cocked her head and listened, absorbed the sound of the fading scream that seemed to stretch and hold itself above familiar noises like the fading note of a guitar string.

She reached for her lamp and pulled the chain. A yellow glow instantly flooded the small room. She flung back the thick shroud of blankets that cocooned her, instantly missing the baking warmth of her electric blanket as she hopped down.

Driven by the ghost of that scream, its echo rattling around in her head like a loose marble, she darted across the room to the window that faced Main Street, her fuzzy socks protecting her from the worst of the cold wood floor. She really needed to ask Sam for a rug.

Pressing hands flat against the bitter-cold glass, she stared out the window at the silent street. Her breath fogged the glass and she wiped it clean with a squeak of her fingertips.

The snow-covered mountains stretched in a wide, jagged outline against the ink-dark night. She scanned the street as if she could somehow see the source of that shriek. There was more light than usual. She looked to the night sky. A full moon stared down at her. Her breath caught in her throat.

Nothing stirred out there in the vast whiteness of the town, and she began to wonder if she'd heard the scream at all. Or had it been in her head, a wisp of a nightmare? Maybe tonight's run hadn't been enough protection, after all.

Surely there'd be light from other windows along the street if it had been real. Mr. Gilberry, the barber across the street, lived in his shop. How could he have slept through that terrible sound? There had to be someone else concerned, curious. Someone . . .

And then she saw him, a shadowy figure out late on a night when everyone else remained warm indoors, snug and safe. When every other soul was in bed, this figure was strolling the sidewalk with a steady, purposeful pace, as if waiting for someone. Or something.

As though he felt her stare, he stopped and turned. His gaze swung up, directly to her window and into her eyes. A small shiver rushed over her. Her chest grew tight, her breath hard to catch. Instantly, she knew him.

Even across the distance his eyes glowed. She felt those indigo eyes like a stroke, a touch against her shivery skin.

Before she had a chance to turn from the window and pretend she didn't notice him, a distant howl floated on the air. Others joined in, the sound awful and eerie.

She tried to peer down the far length of the street to the single blinking stoplight. She didn't know what she expected to see. Wolves parading down the street? The cries were coming from somewhere outside town, much farther away. With another shiver, she looked again to where the stranger stood.

But he was gone.

SIX

More loggers than usual crowded the diner and Darby seriously doubted it was Sam's meatloaf special that lured them in. It was obvious why they were here. The third attack in a month, and this time it was Corey.

No one ate at Sam's who didn't know Corey. She'd been working in the diner since high school. She grew up here. Ironically enough, her death only brought in more customers—as though the diner itself were the scene of the crime. Maggie and Darby could hardly keep up with the orders. Even with all the running she did, she was breathless as she wove between tables.

Corey was the subject on everyone's lips, snatches of conversation filling Darby's ears. She shivered as she recalled her last glimpse of Corey skipping down her porch steps, heading out on her date. And then she shivered again as she recalled *how* she had died. Or at least how people were saying she died.

Corey's body had been found just outside of town. Or rather what was left of her body. The explanation for her slaughter was obvious to everyone. Wolves. What else could it be? What else could have done such damage?

Only Darby wasn't convinced. Darby knew there were other things out there . . . things that did not bear simple explanation.

From the rumble of conversation, she gathered that many of the loggers had abandoned the camps, angry and refusing to return until the wolf threat was "handled."

Darby hurried from table to table, refilling glasses and making sure everyone had what they needed and avoiding pointed questions about Corey. She had no answers to give anyway. And the theory that was starting to form in her head would only get her tossed in a padded room.

She knew she should be grateful for the crowd. The extra tip money was always needed, especially as she was preparing to move on again, but the crowd was a strain. So many people, so many voices. All of it threatened to undo her, to break down her walls, weaken her for a demon's possession.

Her thoughts whirred in her head, mingling with the buzz of the crowded diner. She wished she could just take cover from it all.

She'd give anything for a run, for the steady rhythm of her legs pounding the earth, exorcising her of all troubling thoughts. Maybe after work. She winced and looked out at the diner again, her gaze roaming the full tables. Not likely tonight. Unless she was up for a one a.m. run.

This thought made her shiver again and slide a glance toward the open blinds. Still light out, but it would be a full moon tonight. She wasn't crazy enough to take a midnight jog on a full moon. Even before bodies started turning up, she possessed a healthy respect for those three nights a month when the moon was full.

The door chimed the entrance of more customers and she almost groaned. There was hardly a table left.

She stopped, her mouth drying as she faced the stranger. *Her stranger.*

Calling herself an idiot for thinking of him in such terms, she motioned to the counter and a vacant stool. "Have a seat. Be with you in a second."

From the corner of her eye, she watched as he moved to the counter and settled his lean frame on a stool with easy movements.

"What time you get off, Darby?"

Darby winced, regretting the name tag that let everyone think they could use her name like they were old friends.

"I don't know. We're busy tonight," she replied to a barrel-chested guy who breathed heavily from his mouth. She'd seen him in here several times, though she couldn't remember his name. His interest in her wasn't innocent like the others'. His comments weren't teasing or cajoling. Heavy Breather had dark, empty eyes. She doubted he'd ever had a woman in his life whom he treated with any measure of respect or kindness.

As though to confirm this suspicion, he snatched hold of her wrist as she was collecting his glass for a refill. "How come you never look me in the eye?"

"Come on, let's not do this," she murmured, fighting to keep the edge from her voice. "We've had kind of a rough day around here."

He ignored her request. "I'm paying for good service, right?"

"You're paying for a meal. I'm just here to see you get it." Not the most gracious reply, but Sam never complained about her service before, and her boss's opinion was the only one that mattered to her right now. And if he objected to her attitude, she'd be leaving in a few weeks anyway. Maybe that was making her feel bold.

His dinner companion chuckled. "She told you, Ned."

Ned flushed red.

"Yeah, not so quiet and shy, is she?" His friend shook his head with mirth.

"No, she's not. Guess she's just plain dumb." Ned tugged her closer. "You know that's what everyone says. That you're just a little simple here." He tapped his head right at the temple. "That true? You some retard? Maybe that explains your lack of manners?"

Heat surged through her at his insulting words. "And is that how you get your kicks?" She angled her head. "I mean, if I'm mentally deficient? Does giving a 'retard' a hard time make you feel like a man?"

His friend hooted and tossed back his head. "Bam! She got you there again!"

Darby twisted her wrist, trying to break free. Ned clung tighter than ever, his face flushing a purply red and his breathing falling even harder. "Well, aren't you the smart one after all?"

"Ah, let her go," Ned's friend reprimanded. "You're scaring her."

Ned smiled and she knew that's what he wanted. What would satisfy him. He was that rare breed of man that thrived on intimidation and fear.

"Let her go."

She recognized the deep, cultured tones before she swung a look over her shoulder. *Ah, hell.* A shudder rippled through her. She didn't need him to come to her rescue. She had the situation under control.

The diner quieted—a real feat considering the number of people talking and eating. The clank of glass and silverware stopped. Any moment Sam would poke his head out from the kitchen and then the shit would really hit the fan. He might not mind her less-than-friendly attitude with the customers, but it had never threatened the flow of business before. Sam was a businessman, hoping to retire in the next couple of years. Even he had his limits. She winced. She might be leaving town sooner than planned.

"It's nothing," she growled and motioned him away. "Go away. Sit back down. I'll get to you in a minute."

"He a friend of yours?" Ned demanded.

"No," she replied. That much was true. She didn't even know his name. "Just a customer. Now let me go. I have a job to do."

He released her and rose to his feet, his chair falling back with a crash. "Who are you? You new to these parts? Don't recall I've ever seen you before."

"Who I am is unimportant."

"Aw, Ned. Sit down." Maggie arrived at Darby's side to chastise. "No need to get your feathers ruffled. You haven't even had dessert yet. We've got blueberry pie. On the house. I know it's your favorite. You want whip cream?"

"Yeah, Ned, sit down and stop stirring trouble," someone called out from across the diner.

The vein in Ned's forehead throbbed. He glanced around, a wild look in his dark, moist eyes as he realized the tide was against him.

With a grunt, he dropped back down in his chair.

Maggie squeezed Darby's arm and whispered for her ears alone. "Go on, honey. I'll finish up at this table."

Darby nodded jerkily, bitter resentment filling her throat. "I could have handled it," she muttered as she passed the stranger, careful to keep a safe distance. He smelled good. Clean and piney like the outdoors.

She strode behind the counter and faced him as he reclaimed his stool. The normal sounds of a busy diner resumed as she reached for her pad. She stared down at the paper, intent on not meeting his stare. After yesterday, she knew the mistake that would be.

"What will you have tonight, sir?"

A heavy pause, and then, "I didn't mean to upset you. You just looked like you could use some help."

She breathed through her nose. "I'm not upset,"

she said tightly. "Now. What will you have tonight, sir." *Keep it casual. Don't engage.*

A long moment passed until he finally answered her. "What's good, Darby?" The question fell evenly, mildly, as if he spoke her name all the time. As if they were old friends in the midst of a conversation. *Stupid name tag.*

Her gaze snapped up. Too late, she was caught in the snare of his eyes. They weren't quite glowing. Not like yesterday. But they were still that deep, mesmerizing indigo that sucked her in. Such an impossible color. She couldn't look away.

"Tonight's special is meatloaf."

"And that's what you recommend?"

She paused. "Stick with the cheeseburger. The meatloaf's hit-or-miss and I haven't heard anyone raving about it tonight."

"Sounds good. I'll have that cheeseburger, Darby."

She swallowed. A shiver scraped her skin at the way he said her name, his accents softening it, rolling the *r*. She could love hearing that every day.

Sucking in a breath, she scribbled down his order and turned away. Even when she realized she forgot to ask after his drink, she didn't go back. Not yet. Not until she managed to get a moment for herself. She needed to brace herself before returning to the trap of his eyes.

She turned in his order and seized a waiting tray of food. She worked automatically, like something cold, a robot without thought and emotion, a simply functioning machine, performing the tasks she'd done now thousands of times over the last three years. And she told herself it was enough.

It was surviving.

She didn't let herself consider the emptiness of that thought. The alternative was pain. Death and misery. Not simply to herself but to untold others.

She didn't need the distraction sitting at the counter, the man that screamed danger despite the fact that he had helped her out tonight. *When was he leaving?*

He exuded danger—that was the promise she read in his deep gaze. He tempted her with a break from the emptiness, an escape from her numbing life. In his eyes, she *felt* again and knew that the rush of sensation, hot and cold, good and bad, was not far behind.

She saw his order waiting at the window and stared bleakly at the plate of food that meant her return to him. Taking the plate, she faced the diner, intent on dropping it in front of him and running. Customer service be damned.

"Now that's a feast for the eyes," Maggie said as she came up beside her with a tub of dishes.

"Who?" Darby asked with deliberate vagueness as Maggie poured two coffees.

She snorted. "As if you don't know. He's the reason you're acting all jittery."

"I'm not. Just on edge. Like everyone else."

Maggie sobered. "I'm sad about Corey, too, but don't go blaming some guy because you're upset about Corey. Honey, we're all devastated, but it's times like these when we especially need the comfort of others. Especially when the guy looks that damn good."

Darby lowered her gaze, feeling Maggie's accusation keenly. "He's no one. Just some guy passing through."

Maggie gave a throaty laugh. "Honey, don't you know? Sometimes those are the best types."

Darby paused, thinking, processing this as she observed him reading the local paper, no doubt poring over the details—few as they were—of Corey's slaughter.

She considered Maggie's words and the possible truth in them. Whoever he was, he wasn't from around here. Which meant he wouldn't be staying. So why should she worry so much about him?

He looked up from the paper as she set his plate down in front of him, sliding the ketchup bottle within reach.

"Looks good."

She started to move away but found herself pausing.

He looked at her so intently that there was no way she could move in that moment. He took a bite, chewing slowly, his jaw working.

"Good," he announced, staring at her though, as if he were talking about something else. Not food.

He wiped his mouth with a napkin before tapping the paper with a blunt-tipped finger. "Guess killing those wolves didn't take care of the problem, huh?"

"No," she answered slowly as he took another healthy bite of his burger. Just watching him eat fascinated her. "It didn't. Too bad for Corey."

"Knew her?" he asked.

"Yes. She worked here." She shrugged awkwardly, uncomfortable revealing how affected she was by Corey's death.

He nodded. "I read that in the paper."

"She left a little boy behind."

"That's a shame. Life—" He paused, groping for the right words. He just shook his head. "Life is hard."

Normally this would have come across as dismissive and uncaring. Normally such a cavalier remark would have pissed her off. But she didn't get that vibe from him. He meant what he said because he knew. He knew how hard life could be. He knew firsthand.

She suddenly felt herself hoping he wasn't just passing through. That maybe he was sticking around.

Just as soon as the thought entered her head, she shoved it out with a mental curse. Dangerous, stupid thinking and she knew better.

"Yes, it is hard."

He stared at her, his eyes so deep and peering that she feared he could see inside her to all that was wrong with her. She winced. And that would be a lot.

"You don't think wolves did this," he uttered. A statement, not a question.

He pointed a finger where the paper rested on the counter just in case she was confused about what he was talking about. She wasn't confused. At least not about that. She did wonder why he seemed so interested in what she thought, however. And why was he so interested in the wolf problem? Or rather, the lack of wolf problem.

"I don't know what killed Corey."

"But something did. And you know it's not wolves." He picked up a french fry and bit into it with clean, even teeth. "Interesting. You seem to be the only one around here to share that sentiment."

She glanced around the busy diner, aware that most of the conversation centered around what was going to be done about the wolves. She frowned. If the true threat was what she suspected, there was nothing any of these people could do.

Nothing except bar their doors and pray.

"Don't worry," he said, rising from his stool. He dropped a bill on the counter. "It will all be over soon."

"What do you mean?" She cocked her head.

He hesitated for a moment like he wanted to say something. "Everything will work itself out. Just don't go wandering around at night."

And she knew. He knew what . . . *things* . . . were killing people around here. He suspected the same thing she did. She stared at him, hoping for more elaboration.

He didn't give any. "Good night. Darby."

A small tingle trailed down her spine at the sound of her name on his lips. He seemed to say it almost as an afterthought, like it was something he wanted to experiment pronouncing on his tongue.

As he walked away, she glanced down at the large bill on the counter. "What about your change?" she called, snatching up the money.

He ignored her, continuing out the door and into the cold night.

SEVEN

Niklas walked swiftly through the snow, his booted feet hitting the snow-covered pavement hard, as if each step could jar some sense into his head and remind him of his purpose here.

He cut through the murky, purple air. Night was falling. They were somewhere close, ready to strike again. This time, he'd be there. He lifted his face and breathed in. It was there. A trace of Cyprian and the rest of them. The sickly sweet scent of blood always clung to them and stayed behind on the air.

This was the part he hated. The waiting. The tense holding of his breath as he listened, as he *felt,* scenting the night air, letting his instincts guide him.

He cast a glance over his shoulder at the brightly lit diner fading behind him. A steady stream of people continued to enter the establishment. The usual dinner crowd combined with those morbidly curious about the murdered waitress.

In the future, he would eat somewhere else—if he didn't catch them tonight, of course. He still had tomorrow night though. Certain waitresses were simply far too distracting. He breathed in. He could still smell her. Clean skin and fresh vanilla. He wondered if she tasted the same. He shook his head as if he could dislodge the thought with the fierce motion. She fogged his head with needful thoughts. Thoughts of tangled limbs and sinking himself inside her softness.

He'd thought it was a good idea to eat there considering the pack's latest victim had worked there. He thought he might find out some information, although he probably knew more than anyone else about what exactly was going on. He sure as hell knew that the local wolves hadn't gone on a killing spree. He knew that. And so did she.

Darby. The waitress. She wasn't all that she appeared to be.

As curious as he was about her, as interesting as he found her, he needed to forget her. He was here for one reason and it didn't involve getting entangled with a woman.

He swung his gaze upward. A latticework of branches lining the sidewalk blocked his view of the sky, but he didn't need to see it to know. He could feel it, in the pull and itch of his own flesh, in the hum of his bones. There wasn't much time left.

He located his Hummer at the end of the block. Shooting a glance around his shoulder, he made sure no one was about as he popped his trunk and armed himself with additional weapons.

It was time to hunt.

Closing the trunk, he took off running, diving between buildings. He followed his gut, not using his eyes but that sixth sense he'd possessed since he was sixteen and his world changed forever.

As dusk turned into night, he left the town behind. The blood rushed in his veins as he ran through snow-draped woods. His racing steps were silent in the hush of the forest. An animal of the night, he surrendered to his instincts, all stealth and speed, as dangerous as that which he hunted.

Their howls soon filled the night. Distant, but he followed the sounds, jumping over a frozen creek and vaulting over a five-foot drift of snow.

Their howls grew frenzied and he knew they were closing in on prey. He ran harder, pushing himself. Cocking his head, he inhaled the ripe scent of them on the air and stopped abruptly. Pressing a palm to a nearby tree, he leaned close to the frozen bark and inhaled.

One of them had passed here, brushed against the very spot his hand touched. He dropped to a crouch and assessed the ground. Fresh snow covered it, but he ran fingers through the powdery white anyway, sensing they'd passed over this ground.

Suddenly the howls stopped, swiftly dying in the air. And he knew they'd found their prey.

He took off again, grunting as he vaulted over frozen ground, jumping off a steep craggy hill and landing in a roll until he was on his feet again. The silence told its own story and he ran until his chest hurt. The sound of running water reached his ears.

He broke through the trees and jerked to a halt at its bank. Immediately the tang of freshly spilled blood hit him, powerful and cloying. His gaze zeroed in on the human remains scattered near the side of the partially frozen river. Blood covered the snow for several feet, staining it a deep red so dark it nearly looked black.

He was too late. They'd fed and he was too late. They were gone.

Darby stayed later than usual, helping clean up. But then it had been an unusual night, starting with the news of Corey's death and the diner's sudden surge of business, and then ending with her encounter with the stranger. Another encounter. It seemed odd at this point that she still didn't know his name.

As she headed out the back door, she was too tired to think about heating up a can of soup as she'd planned. Even though her stomach rumbled in hunger, weariness won out. Her bed with its electric blanket tempted her more than the prospect of hot chicken noodle.

As she moved along the short walk to the wooden stairs that led to the upstairs loft, the wind suddenly blew a fierce hiss. The sound reminded her of an angry beast . . . and she'd met a few of those in her life to know. Goose bumps puckered her flesh.

She stopped and looked around. No one else lurked outside. For some reason, she thought about the stranger and his warning to not wander around at night. Not that there was much help for what she was doing—not if she wanted to sleep in her own bed tonight.

Her gaze scanned the diner's back lot. Sam's truck still sat parked beside the Dumpster, empty, its windows dark eyes that only emphasized how alone she felt at this moment. Tall, snow-dappled trees closed around the broken-up concrete, stretching to the night sky. And of course, there was the moon, full and glowing, watchful as an eye in the sky.

She reached for her necklace beneath her sweater, rubbing her fingers over the three pendants, taking comfort in their presence close to her skin. The necklace had been a gift when she turned thirteen and her powers had first begun to assert themselves. Her mother had hoped they wouldn't—had hoped she would be different.

Normal. Normal enough to not attract demons.

Satan's spawn had a particular aversion to milk—the food of life—salt and holy water. Each pendant contained one of these three elements and served to protect her. How much protection it offered, she couldn't say, but she would take whatever help she could get.

And there was the blistering cold of her environment, not to be overlooked. That was perhaps the greatest help of all. Born of the fires of hell, demons could not withstand extreme cold. Their powers of manipulation were always weakest in such climes. So Darby endured living in climates too cold for a demon to thrive.

The wind blew again, the sound it made unearthly as it cut into her face like the sharp pricks of a knife. Almost like a moan.

Awareness settled over her, knotting her shoulders. Her gaze darted around, looking for something where nothing appeared to be. *Appeared.* Her hand tightened around her keys until the relentless metal cut into the tender flesh of her palms. Appearances meant nothing.

Darby knew too well that the world was a place where the wind was sometimes something more than wind. Where shadows weren't always shadows. Where girls who worked in diners were something else, too. Even when they didn't want to be. Even when they would give anything to be something else. Something normal.

Turning, she quickly moved for the stairs, taking two jarring steps at a time, her every instinct commanding her to seek shelter, sanctuary. Her fingers located the right key on the ring in readiness. Her instincts were well honed. She knew to trust them.

"You're sure in a hurry."

He was waiting for her in the shadows of her small porch. He rose from the chair tucked in the corner, blocking her from reaching her door. She should have noticed his heavy breathing sooner. His nose was bright red, and she guessed he had been waiting for a while.

"You think you're something, don't you?" Ned's lip curled as he looked her up and down. He wasn't the first man to get surly with her, but he was the first one to follow her home to harass her. She crossed her arms and returned his stare. For some reason, he failed to intimidate her. When she'd spent half her life contending with demons, this guy hardly registered on her fear radar.

She released a heavy sigh. "You're not going to get out of my way, are you?"

He shook his head, his lips tipping in a cruel smile.

Certain she wasn't going to make it around him and escape into her apartment, she whirled, ready to descend and flee back into the diner.

She didn't make it down one step before she felt a great slam of pressure in her back. Her head snapped on her shoulders as she flew off the steps and landed facedown on the rough concrete at the base of the stairs.

Pain radiated through her body. She lay utterly still for a long moment, a croaked gasp wheezing from her lips as her body absorbed the brunt of impact. Without the cushion of snow, she knew it could have been worse.

Feet pounded heavily on the wood steps above her.

"Oh, did you trip? Gotta be careful on those steps. They can be slippery."

Tripped? Right.

Her hands trembled as she flattened them on the ground. Pain shot through her palms. Wincing, she pulled back and looked at the bleeding scrapes. Apparently the snow hadn't saved her hands from reaching the concrete.

Ignoring the pain, she pushed to her feet, snatching her keys back up from where they had fallen beside her as she did so. "You pushed me," she said in a voice that shook. Oddly, not from terror though. Anger thrummed through her blood.

He nodded. "Kicked, actually."

His thick-soled boots slid to a stop before her.

She stretched to her full height, pulling back her shoulders and ignoring the discomfort in her back from where his boot had struck her.

"What now?" she demanded. "You're going to beat me up? How melodramatic. Go ahead. Let's get this over with."

He tilted his head, studying her as if he'd never seen anything like her before. Fury gleamed in his eyes like a living, glittering beast. "You're afraid. Stop pretending you're not."

Is that what he wanted to see? Her fear. *Idiot.* Fear was nothing. She lived with it every day, waiting for something far worse than him to find her.

She lifted her chin, determined that she not give him the satisfaction. "There's a bully like you in every town on every corner." She smiled at him then, rotating her keys in her hand, readying the largest one for when he came at her again. As she knew he would. Bullies like him were predictable that way.

"Bitch," he growled, his face turning an unflattering purple shade.

He slapped her, but she managed to pull away, taking the force of the blow against her ear rather than her cheek.

Head ringing, she lunged forward and jammed her key into his face, digging the metal in as deep as she could, knowing this was probably the only chance she would have to do him serious injury.

He howled and pulled back. Bright blood flowed freely between his fingers from where she'd gouged him with her key.

Keys still in her hand, she turned and fled up her steps, her goal simple. *Get inside her apartment before he recovered enough to come after her.*

She was at her door, key sliding home in the lock when she heard him pounding up the steps, coming after her like an enraged bull.

Shit!

She released a small cry of relief when she flung the door open, slamming it shut before he reached her. Sliding the lock in place, she took a step back to watch the door shudder beneath the weight of his fists.

Shaking her head, she reached for the phone to call the diner. Sam would be faster than any cops.

Her fingers closed around the phone. She'd just finished dialing when the apartment's single window shattered, the legs of the lawn chair that sat on her porch sticking in through the blinds.

Ned wrestled with the chair, pulling it free with a grunt. Then his arms were there, tearing through the blinds. It wouldn't be long before the lunatic was inside the apartment.

Sam's voice came to her through the phone. "Hello?"

"Sam! It's Darby—" Her voice died abruptly as

Ned suddenly vanished, his wildly groping hands and arms gone. Everything was silent save for Sam's voice in her ear.

Phone pressed against her face, her boss's urgent demands faded away as she took several halting steps closer to the window, her boots crunching over shards of glass.

"Darby? Darby! You there? Answer me!"

"Yeah, I'm here." She finally answered Sam. "It's Ned, the guy from earlier tonight. He's here." Or he was here. "He busted into my apartment."

Sam spit out a quick "On the way."

Darby let the phone drop and covered the last few steps to the window. She peered through the ruined blinds, her chest tight with shallow breaths at what she feared she might find—the very thing that was terrorizing this community.

No one stood on the porch, but a distant sound floated on the winter stillness. *Thunk. Thunk.* Like a hammer pounding into meat. Then a heavy grunt followed.

She stood on tiptoes, trying to see into the back lot. She could only see a panorama of snow-coated trees. And she had to see. Had to know what Sam might be rushing into right now on her behalf.

Unlocking the door, she stepped outside and peered down off the porch, ready to bolt back inside her apartment.

Her heart stopped at the sight that met her eyes.

It was the stranger. The fact that she didn't know his name, or anything about him, seemed almost ridiculous at this point.

But it was him.

He was here, with his fathomless deep eyes and tall, solid form. A ribbon of sensation rippled through her. She fought back a smile.

He stood over an unconscious Ned. He flexed his hands open and shut at his sides, as if he weren't finished . . . as if he still wanted to reach down and choke the last breath of life from the hapless man.

Sam arrived then, skidding to a halt, a dirty frying pan clutched in his hand, grease dripping onto the snow. He scanned the scene, from Darby on the porch to Ned on the ground to the stranger standing so tightly wound above him. The tension ebbed from him.

"Guess you took care of ol' Ned," he muttered, then scowled as his gaze narrowed on the broken window. "Aw, damnit." Lowering the pan, he turned and headed back to the diner. "I'll call the RC. Doubt I'll get a cent for that window out of him though, law or no law."

The stranger's gaze remained fixed on Darby.

She descended the porch, approaching him slowly. "Thanks," she murmured, crossing her arms. Suddenly she was cold. Colder than usual even in this relentless winter.

She scuffed her shoe against the ground, feeling inexplicably nervous. Or maybe embarrassed was more accurate a description. She didn't relish the idea of his having to come to her defense. He probably thought she was one of those weak females who couldn't handle herself. Little did he know just how tough she could be. How resilient she was. How she'd had to be. She'd been on her own for three years. Just herself, staying one step ahead of the demons that would claim her if she dropped her guard and let them.

"You okay?" he asked, his voice gruffer than the last time she heard him speak.

Nodding, she rubbed her scraped palms against her pant legs and winced, having forgotten the injury.

His gaze followed the action and he stepped forward. Without asking, he picked up one of her hands and carefully prodded the abrasions, his touch far gentler than she would have expected.

She glanced down at the still body of her attacker. His barrel chest lifted with easy breaths. At least he was alive.

"Who are you?" She couldn't continue to think of him as "handsome stranger" in her head. Well, she probably *would*, but it'd be nice to have a name, too.

"Niklas," he responded.

"Niklas," she repeated slowly, liking the taste of his name on her lips. It was . . . exotic. Like him.

His thumb moved slowly over her tender palm. Her chest tightened and her stomach knotted and grew queasy all at once. She snatched her hand away. The air around them crackled. She shifted on her feet uncomfortably, achingly aware of him and this attraction that was just . . . *bad*. Wrong. It couldn't happen.

Sam returned then with a groggy-eyed Royal Canadian Mountie who took one look at Ned unconscious in the snow and muttered a profanity. "Ah, hell. Him again?"

"He attacked Darby here." Sam waved at her.

"That so?" The RC scratched his jaw. "That should keep him locked up for a while this time." He looked at Darby. "I'll need a statement."

She nodded.

He sighed as he moved toward the passed-out logger. "Guess we can do it in the morning though. It's late and ass-cold out here. I'll get him in a cell." He glanced at Sam and Niklas. "Mind helping getting him in my car?"

Niklas nodded and hefted the big man into his arms, seemingly with little effort. Darby felt her mouth sag.

The officer gawked for a moment before leading

the way around the building. Darby stood there, watching them disappear, still feeling the touch of his hand on hers. Tingles rippled up her arm.

"Hey, Darby. I'll get some cardboard for that window."

She started at Sam's voice. She almost forgot he was still standing next to her.

He continued, "It'll have to do until tomorrow. You're welcome to stay the night with me and Vera—"

"No, thanks," she replied automatically. Staying overnight with two other souls, potentially endangering them . . . it was out of the question. Especially Sam and his wife. They were good people and had been nothing but kind to her.

"Suit yourself." Sam left and returned moments later with some broken-down boxes. Together they taped them over her window. She looked over her shoulder every now and then, half expecting, half hoping for Niklas to return. Perhaps even dreading it a little bit. Because she shouldn't want him to come back. She was grateful for his help, but really, he should just stay away.

"That should do it." Sam stepped back to inspect their handiwork. "Sure you'll be okay? There'll still be a draft."

"Got the electric blanket."

Sam nodded. "Well, g'night."

He clomped down the wooden steps and she shut the door, not bothering to remove her coat. The room wasn't much warmer than the air outside. She might have to sleep in her heavy parka.

She put the kettle on to boil and found herself pacing the small space of her kitchen, rubbing the back of her neck with anxious fingers.

Suddenly, she felt wired. Sucking in her breath, she undressed and slipped into a pair of flannel pajamas, donning the thickest pair of fuzzy socks she owned. She moved to the sink and turned on the warm water to rinse her palms, sighing with pleasure.

A knock sounded as she was patting her hands dry. Her heart jumped. She knew who it was before she looked through the peephole.

Opening the door to a blast of cold air, she trained her expression into one of cool reserve as she prepared to face her knight in shining armor for the night.

The last thing she expected to see was the cold fury gleaming in his indigo eyes. "What in hell do you think you're doing?" he growled.

Behind her, the whistle to the kettle blew.

EIGHT

Darby gaped at him. "Excuse me?"

Niklas looked particularly displeased as he stared down at her. "What do you think you are doing?"

"Um." She glanced over her shoulder at the rattling kettle. "Making some hot chocolate."

"Why are you even here?" He glanced disgustedly at the window covered in cardboard, apparently unbothered by the screeching kettle. "You can't mean to stay the night here. You'll freeze."

She moved into the kitchen and removed the kettle from the burner. "I have an electric blanket."

"You've got to be kidding. Your boss expects you to—"

"No. Sam invited me to stay the night with him and his wife."

"Then why didn't you?"

"Because I'm fine," she snapped, getting annoyed. She couldn't explain that she couldn't fall asleep with others nearby—that she was a danger to them. And what business was it of his anyway? "It's just for one night. He'll repair the window tomorrow."

"One night is all it takes to freeze to death. And can you make it any easier for . . ."

"For what?" she pressed, her eyes scanning him intently. Was this it? Would he say what he knew? Would he admit to possessing knowledge that matched her own suspicions?

"Can you make it any easier for danger to find you?" he finished, his eyes glowing again.

She pulled back, her gaze narrowing. "What are you talking about? Truly? Stop being vague." She spoke quietly, almost as if she didn't want the night to overhear her words.

Deep in her bones, she felt there was more to this man. A lot more. Things he knew that she knew, too. They were toeing a dangerous line, dancing around each other with their secrets.

"There are all kinds of things that could harm a woman alone. And you're more vulnerable than most." He motioned to the boarded-up window, but she noticed that his gaze drifted, moved to her front window, out at the sky, to the full moon hanging low on the night.

"What business is it of yours anyway?"

At this, he stared at her, a cold shutter falling over his gaze as the truth of her question drilled deep.

"What do you care?" she demanded, pushing the point, feeling she was close. Close to pushing him away. Close to running him off for good. As much as the thought of this stung her, she charged ahead, needing to drive him away. "You don't know me. I don't know you."

A heavy beat of silence stretched between them, strained and uncomfortable.

He inhaled. "You're right." He moved toward the door.

She couldn't make herself move or speak. She had to see him leave, had to watch him walk away even as an inexplicable ache built in her chest. She watched the broad shoulders, the rigid set of his spine and embraced that she'd never have him or any other man ever again.

She'd said the words, done everything to get him to leave her alone—even as her heart, her body willed him to stay, willed him to come closer. To touch her as he had earlier with that simple brush of his fingers. To touch her *more* than that. To fill the ache of loneliness gnawing away at her.

Weak, she knew, and foolish and selfish. But that was how she felt. Thankfully only how she *felt*. She gave nothing away, no outward sign, no indication that she wanted him to do any of those things. She was responsible, at least.

What choice do you have?

He stopped then, turned back and stared at her, pinned her with his deep gaze. She forgot how to breathe beneath that intense stare, both afraid and hopeful that he would read her want, her need.

"Go," she whispered, inwardly cringing at the pathetic whisper of her voice. Hardly convincing.

He angled his head, the light in his eyes intensifying the longer he stared, taking her apart piece by piece, opening her up to see what it was she hid inside . . . who she was.

He moved before she could process it. A blur and rush of wind that bewildered her.

Before she had time to process just what happened, he was in front of her, hauling her into his arms, lifting her off her feet as he claimed her mouth. Heat. That was her first impression as he enveloped her. Encompassing heat and male strength.

Shock rippled through her at the sensation of his mouth on hers. She gasped and he took advantage, deepening the kiss, forcing her mouth open for his slanting lips.

His lips were warm like the rest of him. They moved firmly, expertly, robbing her of all will as he pushed deeper inside her apartment, backing her up against a wall.

Her hands hovered for a moment at her sides, warring with her weakening will. She should push him away, end this insanity before it went further. And yet she failed to do any of that.

With the fleeting thought that she really should know better than to do this flashing across her mind, she seized his shoulders. She was lost. There was no going back. She clung to him, pressing against him as their mouths fused, moving feverishly, tasting and sucking.

She yanked down the zipper of his bulky coat and slid her hands inside, skimming her palms over his chest, his dark sweater warm and soft and tantalizing against her palms, only a single barrier separating her from his firm chest, and she wanted to be rid of it. His heart thudded swiftly beneath her exploring hands and she moaned into his mouth, desperate for his flesh on hers, for an answer to the ache in her belly.

His hands cupped her face and the gesture struck her as both tender and desperate. Her knees trembled. Without the wall at her back and his hard body at her front, she doubted whether she could remain standing.

He slid one hand down her throat in a fiery trail and covered her breast through her flannel top. She whimpered against his mouth and surged shamelessly against that hand.

It wasn't enough. Not nearly enough. Not after the lonely years. Not after one taste of him.

This is what she'd wanted from the first moment she ran into him outside the store. Since the instant she'd glimpsed his hand and her entire body had ignited.

He crowded her, pressing closer, overwhelming her senses. She gasped raggedly when he broke their fused lips. His lips singed her cheek, skimming toward her ear, fanning heat and moist kisses there that left her panting.

He lifted his head. Heart hammering wildly in her chest, she glanced up only to find his gaze fixed on her face, his eyes searching, scanning every nuance, missing nothing.

He looked at her strangely, his eyes feverish, intense, consuming. As though he had never seen anything quite like her before. Her chest tightened.

Reaching out, he caught a lock of her hair. Studying the red strands, he rubbed them experimentally between his fingers. Dropping her hair, he ran the back of his fingers down her cheek, igniting a trail in their wake.

Her breath caught in her throat, trapped, frozen within her like a bird in the face of its predator. And like prey, she looked away, dropped her gaze, wishing he would step away from her, wishing it with the same desperation that she hoped he would not.

He inhaled deeply next to her cheek. "You smell so sweet. Like vanilla."

"It's my lotion," she murmured lamely, her gaze returning to him, brushing his chin, his mouth, his nose, until she locked eyes with him again.

He watched her with fierce relentlessness. She felt as if his gaze alone could strip away everything, all her barriers, reveal all her secrets, all that she hid from the world. She shivered.

"What are you?" he murmured, his voice a wisp of heat on the air, so close he scorched her bruised lips.

Closing her eyes tightly, she shook her head, panicked that he should see anything at all when he looked at her. Anything close to the truth.

"N-nothing," she choked.

"Oh, no," he returned, his voice quiet and confident and much too close as he tucked a strand of hair behind her ear, his thumb caressing her earlobe in a deft, sensual stroke. "You're definitely . . . *something*."

His lips came back down on hers again. She moaned into his mouth and leaned into him. His hand found her breast again.

She didn't know what burned hotter, his lips on her or the imprint of his hand on her aching breast. And then there was her blood. It baked in her veins, drove her to a frenzy. She buried her hands in his hair and pulled his mouth closer, deepened their kiss with a ferocity that might have frightened her if she had let rational thought even enter her head.

She was beyond rational thinking.

She ravaged his mouth, biting, licking, sucking. She unleashed herself, unleashed everything she had denied and hidden away for the last three years. And he gave it all back to her, met her every lick, her every kiss and nip. He took and seized, his mouth and hands fierce and thorough. Everywhere.

A sob rose in her throat as he buried his warm face in her throat, sucking on the stretched cord there. His teeth scored her sensitive flesh. She trembled from the inside out, her fingers digging into his shoulders, clinging . . .

He growled, the dark sound vibrating against her skin.

She stilled at the deep animal sound, startled and a little frightened.

What the hell was that?

The noise didn't even sound . . . *human. He* didn't. He sounded like, like . . .

He wrenched away from her, his hands hard on her arms, holding her away from him as if he didn't trust himself to have her near him.

His chest heaved, ragged breaths tripping from his mouth. He closed his shining eyes in a savage blink, torment etched into his face.

Her own gasping breath filled her ears. She watched him intently, trying to make sense of what she'd heard, of what she read in his face, what she saw there in every anguished line and angle . . . of the impossible thought skittering through her head.

He opened his eyes. They glowed with that eerie light again. He looked at her with such stark longing that all fear melted away. For a moment, she thought he would pull her back into his arms and devour her . . . finish what they started. What she wanted.

But no. Instead, he flung her away as if the touch of her burned his hands. He was gone so quickly, she hardly saw him leave. There one moment and then gone the next. She blinked and brushed a shaking hand to her lips. *What just happened?*

She moved to the door and looked out, but he was already gone. *So much for his worrying about her staying the night alone in an apartment with a broken window.*

Her shaking fingers traveled from her bruised lips to her throat, still hot and tender from his kisses. Her body throbbed, ached. Freezing to death wouldn't be problem tonight. She doubted she would cool down any time soon. Not with the memory of him to warm her.

NINE

Niklas stood just out of sight, beneath a canopy of snow-draped trees behind the diner. Branches creaked in the arctic wind as he watched Darby close the door of her apartment. His breathing had yet to slow. His hands curled tightly at his sides.

A low growl burned at the back of his throat, dark and primal—the part of himself he couldn't deny, as much as he loathed it. The beast in him simmered just beneath his rippling skin, fighting to burst free. For the first time in years, since he'd first turned, he'd doubted his ability to keep himself in check—to keep the beast away.

She did that to him. *Darby*. Damn her. He shook his head, bewildered. No female had ever had that effect on him before. Good thing he'd be gone soon. Far from her.

He sensed the pack was close. He could feel them on the air, in his shuddering skin, in his over-warmed blood. He didn't need the trail of bodies they left to tell him that they were nearby.

Their numbers were small—had dwindled since he first began hunting them. This time, he'd have them. He'd have them all, but most important, Cyprian would be his.

Cyprian, who stole his mother and condemned her to hell. The bastard took everything from Niklas and he would pay for it.

He leaned back against a tree. No more chasing them from city to city, country to country, continent to continent. This was it. No matter how enticing, he wouldn't let himself be distracted by a piece of ass. He flinched even as he thought the words. He hardly knew Darby, but he didn't like thinking of her that way. How was it she had come to mean something to him? He didn't know her and yet he craved her.

Even knowing he had to keep her at arm's length, he still found himself lingering beneath the trees. She was vulnerable to more than the cold. A distant howl floated on the night as if to prove that point. His impulse was to shove off from the tree and hunt down that sound, pursue it until he found Cyprian. But another part of him couldn't tear himself away. He couldn't leave her unprotected. Especially on a full moon.

He settled back against the tree. Crossing his arms, he trained his gaze on the boarded-up window and tried not to focus too intently on the mental images he had of the woman preparing for bed behind that flimsy barrier.

After her visit to the RC the following morning, where she gave her statement, Darby fell back into her usual pattern. Or at least she tried to. She figured she had a few more weeks in this town before it was time to move on yet again, before the weather warmed up and it became too dangerous to stay.

A part of her wanted to linger. Sam let her stay in the apartment for practically nothing. She wouldn't find an arrangement this good in the next town. She never had before. She'd lived in some rat holes previously, living off crackers and ramen noodles. And everyone here cared about her . . . Maggie, Sam, Vera. And as much as she didn't want to, she cared about them, too.

This town had been different from the others where she'd been able to lose herself in the monotony of work. The long hours waitressing tables didn't lull her as it usually did. She felt as if she had woken from a lengthy sleep. And then there was *him*. And that kiss.

As she went about the day, her gaze constantly flew to the door every time she heard it chime, searching, hoping . . .

Only it was never Niklas. Maybe he'd moved

on. And her heart sank at the thought of this. No matter how she told herself to snap out of it, the thought that he was gone, that her first taste of excitement in years had vanished and her life had returned to its same dull emptiness depressed her. She wished she'd never laid eyes on him—wished that she hadn't woken up to how thrilling life could be again.

With a shake of her head, she tried once again to numb herself with the familiar tasks of the job, taking orders, carrying out trays laden with food, refilling glasses. The diner was still crowded with men refusing to go out to the camps until the wolf problem was handled. They came in at breakfast and stayed, talking over their coffees. A little before lunch the door chimed loudly.

A teenage boy stood on the threshold, letting the cold air inside. A customer shouted at him to shut the door. He ignored the complaint, announcing loudly in a cracking voice, "They found another body down by the river!"

Darby's heart sank as she thought of the distant howls she'd heard the night before as she lay in her bed.

Chairs scraped as everyone poured out of the diner to investigate this latest development.

Maggie shouted at a few of them to pay their bills, snapping a dish towel after them.

Darby sighed and sank onto a stool at the counter as the diner emptied. Sam cursed from the kitchen window.

"Why don't you round up the dishes and then take your lunch break?" he suggested to Darby. "Something tells me we'll be empty for the next few hours."

"Sure, Sam."

"Oh, and I'll get to that window this afternoon. Don't want you sleeping in there another night like that."

Nodding, she made quick work of busing tables. Maggie soon joined her—her cheeks flushed from her quick run outside. She muttered under her breath about having to run down customers to pay their bills.

"What's this world coming to when you think it's okay to steal food? It's a thankless job, Darby. You need to get out before it ruins your legs. Not to mention your face." She motioned to her sagging jowls. "Think I'd have wrinkles like this if I'd married myself a doctor and played tennis twice a week and got pedicures every month? No sirree. Instead I look like this—a saddlebag with eyes."

"Are there lots of doctors around here? Or tennis courts?" Darby couldn't help asking, her lips curling in a teasing smile.

"Go ahead and laugh, girl. No one said I had

to stay in this town, but I did. If you know what's good for you, you'll get out. Especially now, with wolves making a meal out of everyone . . ." She paused, shaking her head. Turning, she looked out the window. Her heavily lined faced stared out at the world with a hopelessness that Darby felt echo inside herself. Everything was white or gray. Snow and the drab colors of the buildings surrounding them. "Don't know why anyone would want to stay here."

Darby's teasing smile slipped from her face. Without comment, she moved into the kitchen and changed her shoes. Stepping outside into the cold, she tromped around to the back of the diner, her mind drifting to whatever poor dead soul was mauled last night.

Maybe she needed to go ahead and leave now before the next dead body showed up. Halfway up the wood steps, she stopped and gawked at the sight before her.

The pieces of cardboard covering her window were gone. A new window glinted at her, the glass clean and clear as ice. She looked over her shoulder as if she would see someone there who could explain this to her. She knew Sam hadn't done it—he wouldn't have had the time. Who then? The RC? He hadn't mentioned anything to her this morning in his office.

Niklas's face materialized in her mind. Had he done this? She turned in a small circle, scanning the back lot of the diner as if she would find him out there.

Nothing. He wasn't around. She didn't see him . . . didn't feel him. And for some reason she was beginning to suspect she had the ability to sense him—whoever, *whatever* he was. He was no ordinary man. Ironic, considering she was no ordinary woman. And he knew that. He'd asked her *what* she was last night like he knew she was something else. She hadn't forgotten the strangeness of that question.

Shaking her head, she turned back around and unlocked her apartment. Once inside, she was struck by how warm it was. *Very* warm. She glanced around and stopped cold at the sight of the brand-new heater. Holding out a hand, she wiggled her fingers in front of it, letting the gust of warm air blow over her chilled flesh.

He did this. She knew it. A deep smile curved her mouth.

He might have torn himself away from her last night and practically run away . . . but he'd come back and done this for her. She shook her head, still bewildered as to why.

Moving to the window, she stared outside again. She knew she wouldn't see him there, but that didn't stop the hope from springing in her heart. Wrong or right, she wanted to see him again. Even if it was only for one night. One more kiss.

Face it, Darby. You want more than another kiss from the man . . . from whatever he was.

She sucked in a bracing breath and reminded herself that nothing had changed. She was still a woman who couldn't stay anywhere too long, still couldn't get involved with anyone. She was too unpredictable, too dangerous.

The fact that he might be just as dangerous, maybe even more dangerous, didn't make it okay for her to be around him.

THE DINER WAS PACKED later that evening, the usual crowd of loggers and locals all talking about the body found down by the river—Jeremiah Hollis, a foreman for one of the camps who hadn't gone on strike and had stayed behind.

Darby dropped a plate in front of a little girl, a welcome change from the burly men packing the place tonight. Her eyes lit up at the sight of the grilled cheese and golden french fries. She was maybe seven years old, sweet-faced with a cloud of brown hair that seemed to float around her shoulders. A small beauty mark dotted the skin just below her left eye, drawing attention to the green-blue of her eyes.

Darby watched as the girl scooted her little fort of carefully arranged sugar packets to the side, her tiny fingers precise and cautious as she maneuvered the pink and blue packets to make room for her plate.

Darby cocked her head, watching in bemusement, feeling a flash of memory of herself somewhere else doing the same thing. Another time and place. She remembered sitting beside her mother as they ordered breakfast at their favorite neighborhood diner.

Her mother wasn't much of a cook. They ate at that diner several nights a week. Maybe that's why Darby gravitated to diners. They were a familiar comfort. Home in many ways.

Her gaze drifted to the woman in the booth, the girl's mother. Looking at her, it was like seeing her mother again—the sunken eyes, shadowed and dim from lack of sleep, from constant worry and fear. Here sat another soul beaten and battered from life.

It was as though she had been given a glimpse into her past and a chord of empathy struck deep inside her.

Shaking off the troubling musings, she complimented the little girl, "Aren't you pretty?"

The girl ducked her head coyly against her mother's shoulder and played with a fry.

"What do you say, Aimee?"

The girl's "Thank you" was barely audible, lost in the thick cowl of her purple sweater.

Darby glanced to the mother. Close to Darby's own age, she was pale with tired and beaten eyes. The tabletop in front of her was empty.

"Are you sure you don't want to order something?" Darby asked gently.

"No, I'm fine. Thank you." Her eyes dipped, avoiding Darby's gaze, as if afraid to let Darby see the truth there. That she wasn't fine. That she was hungry but could only pay for one meal.

"From out of town?" By now Darby recognized most of the locals.

"Yes. We're waiting on the bus. Got some time to kill."

"I'm going to see my grandma!" the little girl piped up, bouncing in the red vinyl booth. "Daddy has a new lady friend staying with him and there isn't enough room for us anymore."

The child declared this openly, honestly, her wide eyes reflecting no awareness that this was wrong . . . that a father shouldn't kick his wife and child to the curb for his new "lady friend."

A painful lump formed in Darby's throat. She knew from firsthand experience that a father never *should* do that. But fathers did. Fathers left all the time when things got too tough or the fun simply ran out.

"Aimee," the young mother chided, color staining her wan face as she folded the little girl's hand into her own.

Empathy filled Darby's heart for the pair. Well, at least they had each other . . . and someplace to go. And maybe a helping hand along the way.

With a brusque nod that she hoped disguised the sudden emotion she felt, she ripped off the check and set it down on the table. "Here you go." She smiled at Aimee. "Enjoy your dinner."

Walking back to the kitchen, she grabbed a bowl from the towering stack. In one smooth move, she poured a good portion of beef vegetable soup from the large electric pot, taking satisfaction at the sight of healthy chunks of potatoes, carrots and sirloin. Sam's soups were definitely hearty. Perfect fare in this weather. She'd eaten more than her share.

Weaving through tables, she stopped and deposited the bowl in front of the young mother. She laid a napkin and spoon down, too.

The woman blinked as if coming awake from a daze and looked from the bowl to Darby. Her thin shoulders stiffened. "I didn't order this."

"We have plenty of it . . . and we're throwing it out after tonight, so you might as well enjoy some."

The woman glanced down at the steaming

bowl, looking torn, the hollows of her cheeks more pronounced as she weighed the price of her pride versus the need for food in her belly.

"Go on," Darby prompted. "Hate for good food to go to waste." She flicked a glance at the girl munching happily on her grilled cheese, her innocent eyes drifting between her mother and Darby. "You need your strength." She didn't say it, but her thoughts came across loud and clear. *Your daughter needs you strong.*

"Thank you," she murmured, her voice shaky as she picked up her spoon.

With a nod, Darby turned and went about her work. She returned later, happy to see the soup bowl empty.

"That was very good." The young mother pushed long bangs in need of a trim from her eyes.

Darby removed the bowl. "Sam's a great cook. Especially his goulash. You ever stop this way again, be sure to try it. Will give you a whole new perspective on goulash."

"I'll do that." She smiled. "Do I pay you here or—?"

"Yeah, you can pay me."

Darby tucked a strand of hair behind her ear and waited as the woman dug into her tiny coin purse. She handed some badly creased and wadded bills to Darby. Their fingers brushed and a jolt of electricity passed into Darby at the contact—a sharp current of energy she hadn't felt in a long time. Because she wanted it that way. She'd worked hard, done everything in her power to make certain that moments like this were kept to a minimum.

She gasped, her entire body locking up tight, freezing motionless. Suddenly she was somewhere else. A hazy shadowland. Dusk blanketed the fading day. Snow covered the ground. Sleeping buildings, already closed for the day, watched with darkened windows for eyes as little Aimee was there, walking hand in hand with her mother. Blurry figures approached, men and yet not. Something more. Something else.

Creatures of nightmares. Eyes like glowing pewter. They moved so fast, streaks on the air.

Darby was there, a mere spectator, unable to help, unable to do anything but watch everything from an angle somewhere above them.

They sprang. Their silver eyes flashed on the air. The mother and daughter didn't stand a chance against them. These were predators. *Lycans*. They swept the mother and daughter off their feet in a move so terrible and beautiful it seemed choreographed, something they had done countless times. The creatures folded them into their arms and whisked them away before they even had a chance to scream.

But Darby did. She let loose a choking sound. The cry strangled in her throat as she returned to herself in the middle of the diner, shaking where she stood in the bright fluorescent light, clutching the other woman's hand in a death grip, witness to her murder. Hers and Aimee's. Murders that had yet to occur. Murders that were going to happen.

Unless she did something about it.

TEN

Darby regained her breath and blinked several times, looking around cautiously, assessing her surroundings to see if she'd drawn attention to herself. Most of the customers continued to eat and talk at their tables, only a few looked at her oddly, but they were the least of her worries. Freaking out a few customers would be unfortunate, but attracting a demon . . .

She shivered and waited to see if her magic had attracted one of the bastards.

After a moment, she released her breath and let herself feel safe again, relieved. Demons hadn't found her. Apparently the cold climate had done its work, repelling the creatures. She was safe from their tormenting influence. For now.

The woman tugged her hand free of Darby's grip. Until that moment Darby didn't realize she still clung to her.

"Let me go," she growled, rubbing at the red marks Darby left on her hand.

Darby winced. "Sorry about that."

"What's wrong with you?" she demanded, her eyes bright with anger.

If she only knew. Darby studied the woman, seeing her as she'd seen her in her vision, the stark terror in her eyes moments before was taken.

She took a deep breath. "I—I'm sorry." *How could she explain what just happened*? Darby glanced around to see that several more customers were looking at her now. She'd seen those expressions before. The look that said *freak*. She didn't make it through junior high school without her visions choosing the most inopportune times to strike. The seventh-grade musical, the eighth-grade Spring Fling. Oh, she'd never forget that time during volleyball tryouts. Safe to say, she didn't make the team that year—or ever again. Each episode sank her farther and farther into social death.

The woman slid out from the booth and bundled Aimee back into her coat and hat, all the while sending uneasy glances to Darby, like she was a lunatic that might spring at her any moment.

Still shaking from the aftermath of her vision, Darby watched them, the need to do something to help them rising up inside her, overwhelming her.

Her mother had warned her about that, told her

again and again that she mustn't use her powers and attract demons. No matter the purpose. Still, she couldn't hold silent. "You can't go out there."

The woman increased her movements, gracelessly fumbling with Aimee's zipper. Darby glanced out the diner window, her chest tightening at the fading light. Dusk was nearly upon them. "You can't go out there," she repeated in a stronger voice.

The young mother rose to her feet and leveled a frosty glare at Darby. "You need to back off."

Darby tried for a coaxing tone. "Look, I'm sorry. What's your name?" Maybe if she spoke her name, she would come across as friendlier.

The woman didn't appear inclined to answer. She pressed her lips into a thin line.

"Pam," Aimee cheerfully volunteered, unaware of the tension swirling around them. "Her name is Pam."

"Aimee! C'mon," Grabbing her daughter and purse, Pam whirled around.

Darby lunged after her and grabbed her arm. "Stop. Wait. You're in danger. Don't go out there, Pam. I saw—I saw something—"

Pam twisted her arm free. "Freak! Leave us alone."

Freak.

The word *still* stung. Even now. Even though

she'd heard it countless times, it still had the power to wound. Her hand dropped from Pam's arm.

"Darby," Sam called her name from the counter, frowning at her.

The bell at the door chimed their departure. When Darby looked back, they were gone, diving out into the street. She moved toward the door.

"Darby!" Sam called, frowning at her through the kitchen window. "What's going on?"

She looked from Sam and out the smudged glass door to the retreating figures. There was no choice. She had to do something. Had to try, had to help. Not about to let the pair of them get too far away, she snatched a coat off the rack by the door, not caring who it belonged to, and dove out into the bite of winter.

Their figures were already fading down the street in the lightly falling snow as they walked briskly toward the bus station at the center of town.

Darby shouted into the wind, calling after them.

Pam looked over her shoulder and then picked up her pace, practically dragging her daughter along. Darby increased her own pace, forgetting that she'd vowed to keep her head low, to never use her powers, even if it meant ignoring others in need.

Such a promise had made perfect sense at the time. Sure, she could help a few, but to what end?

Potentially losing herself to a demon? Letting a demon manipulate her into doing terrible things? The risk was too great.

But this vision had struck her unsolicited, and she could not ignore it—or the chance to save the two souls fleeing her as if *she* were the danger. She had to help them.

As far as she could tell, no demons had shown up to try and claim her for the episode back at the diner. Her visions often acted as a kind of signal, alerting demons to her location. Apparently she'd gone undetected—or it was too cold for any demon to make an appearance. Whatever the case, maybe this was supposed to happen. Maybe she was supposed to save them.

"Stop! Wait," she shouted as they turned off the main sidewalk. She ran harder, her feet striking deeply into the snow-caked sidewalk.

Darby guessed that Pam was trying to lose her, but getting off the town's main street wasn't a smart move. Her gut knotted. *Not a good move.* She knew it because she knew they had been in a deserted alley in her vision.

Following, she turned and stared down the narrow stretch of broken-up concrete that ran between two brick buildings.

She stilled at the mouth of the alley. Pam and Aimee were out of sight, but the alley was long.

She knew they couldn't have reached its end and turned down the other street yet. They were still here. Close.

"Hello?" she called, shaking off her hesitation. Dusk was close. There wasn't much time. Streaks of fading sunlight colored the air. Everything was as she'd seen in her vision. The narrow alley, the dark buildings pressing close. The only things missing were the silver-eyed men. *Men.* They were hardly that.

"Please come out. I—I think . . . You're in trouble. I just want to help. I'm not going to hurt you."

A small whisper reached her ears, followed by a quick hushing sound. Darby stopped before a Dumpster, its odor ripe and foul on the air. A pair of pink sneakers peeked around one edge.

She rounded the Dumpster and confronted them. The mother clutched Aimee close to her side, both arms wrapped fiercely around her small frame.

Darby held both hands up in front of her. "Please. Just come back to the diner with me. Nothing will happen to you there."

Pam shook her head, her eyes wide and fearful, and Darby called herself every kind of idiot for being the one to put that fear there. She'd handled this badly. She should have never let the mother and daughter leave the diner. Even if she had to create a scene she should have made certain they stayed far from this alley.

"We don't want any trouble," Pam whispered, and Darby heard what she wasn't saying in that simple statement. *All I've known is trouble and fear in my life. I don't want anymore. Please, no more.* "We've got a bus to catch."

"There will be another bus," Darby insisted and looked down at the girl. "You didn't get any cake? Wouldn't you like a slice of chocolate cake, Aimee?" She wasn't above manipulating the child to help them.

Aimee nodded and looked hopefully toward her mother. "Momma?"

Her mother shook her head no.

"Please, Momma. Let's go back to the diner." Aimee's voice quavered the slightest bit, and Darby knew she had gained the child's trust at least.

Pam sighed. "Okay." Her gaze cut back to Darby, still distrustful. "We'll go back to the diner and then you can explain yourself. In front of witnesses."

A relieved whoosh of air rushed from her. She nodded. "Good."

Then there was the slightest change in the air. Subtle as the wind. A noise emerged. *Tap, tap, tap.* It took her a moment to process the sound for what it was. The steady fall of footsteps.

Her pulse jackknifed against her throat. She swung around and saw two men, approaching the same way she'd entered the alley. With a sinking sensation, Darby knew they'd been out there, stalking prey in the town. She knew that they'd seen the three of them rush into this alley. Easy pickings.

They were garbed in dark winter attire and walked with an animal stealth, their steps deceptively slow, silent as wind—but she knew they could spring like a lion in the grass. She knew because she knew what they were. She'd seen them in her head only minutes ago.

Even in the gloom of the alley, with distance between them, the eerie pewter of their eyes drilled into her, marked them instantly as the monsters she knew them to be.

There'd been four in her vision. She whipped around, seeing only these two as of yet. But she knew the others were coming. Her skin prickled. They'd be here soon.

"We have to go now," she growled in a feverish rush of words, hoping, believing there was still a chance as long as the other two lycans hadn't arrived.

Beyond all coaxing, she snatched Pam by the arm and forced her to move. Pam glanced at the menacing pair. Weirdly enough it seemed that recognition flickered in her eyes. Even though she couldn't suspect what they truly were, she evidently recognized a predator when she saw one.

With a fearful nod, Pam tucked her daughter to her side and turned with Darby to flee in the other direction.

They moved only one step before two more figures appeared at that far end of the alley, boxing them in. They were trapped. There was no moving ahead and no going back.

Darby's pulse hammered fast and hard against her neck. Her fingers dug hard into Pam's arm. She relaxed her grip when she heard her whimper.

"Who are they?" Pam demanded in a low voice. "What do they want?"

Darby glanced around, looking for a weapon, anything to use to defend them. A two-by-four with some nails jutting out one end was piled against the side of the building with other debris. She seized hold of it. It wouldn't kill any of them—she knew enough about lycans to know that—but it was something.

She flexed her hand around the rough, splintery wood. Maybe it would be enough to injure one of the bastards . . . or at least make them work hard for their dinner. Time was of the essence. Lycans had remained undiscovered by most of the world for this long because of their discretion and because they were good at what they did—kill.

She knew they wouldn't want to mess around with them too long. Soon the moon would ride high, and they wouldn't want to linger in the relative open once they transitioned and risk exposure.

She slapped the wood against her hand, trying to look tougher than she felt.

One of the lycans cocked his head and studied her curiously with his coldly handsome face. She was certain he turned heads and lured many to their deaths with those deep-set, mesmerizing eyes, freakishly silver or not. He pushed his hood back from his head to reveal a head full of dark blond dreadlocks. "Aren't you the feisty one?"

Darby positioned herself sideways, looking back and forth between each pair. "We're not going to make it easy. You better go find a meal somewhere else."

The woman close to her head made a strangling sound, clearly frightened by Darby's words.

"Meal?" Dreadlocks asked with genuine surprise. "What an interesting choice of words. Why would you say that? We're just lost. Thought you could help set us on the right path."

One lycan dove for her in a blur. Darby swung,

ready. He howled in agony as she met him upside the head with the nailed end.

He staggered back, clutching his bleeding face and screeching.

One of his brethren chided, "Oh, shut up, Marcus. You'll heal."

"That bitch!" he shrieked, pulling back a hand to stare at his blood there. "She stuck a nail in my face!"

Dreads continued to stare at Darby as if he didn't know what to make of her.

"Better move on and hunt somewhere else. I'm just gonna drag this out for you," she warned with more bravado than she felt. Adrenaline burned through her veins, keeping her alert, ready. "It's almost dark," she reminded, jerking the two-by-four in her hands skyward. "You don't want to dawdle here, do you?"

Dreads shook his head and announced in a marveling voice, "You know who we are."

"Yeah. I know." She nodded. "So get the hell out of here."

"Oh, no, I can't do that. You're much too interesting. Cyprian will want to speak to you."

Before she could blink he was on her. He was fast. Faster than the other one. Too fast for her. He wrenched the two-by-four from her fingers and slammed her to the ground. Pain exploded in the back of her head. Spots danced before her eyes and for one moment she thought she was going to black out.

The other three grabbed Aimee and Pam, slapping hands over their mouths to silence their screams.

Dreads pushed his face close, his lips grazing her cheek as he spoke. "Your scent . . . you don't smell human. What are you?"

She grunted, struggling to break free.

"Hurry, Devon. We don't have much time."

Devon. Almost like *demon*. Fitting. These creatures weren't that much different from the demons that wanted to claim her soul.

"Not talking? Pity. You will." A warm chuckle puffed from his lips. "You will." He hauled her to her feet in one smooth move.

She spit in his face, strangely not frightened. Not for herself anyway. She was tired of being afraid, she realized. Tired of running.

He smiled, wiping his face. "That's not nice. Why don't you like me?" His gaze flicked over her. "I like you. We're going to be friends, you and I." Her face must have revealed some of her revulsion. He chuckled. "Come." He flicked another glance upward. "You're right. It's almost moonrise."

ELEVEN

They were transported quickly, thrown into the back of a van without any windows—a lightless box. A relentless cold crept into her body from the hard metal floor, seeping through her heavy garments and into her very bones.

In the dark, Darby's senses heightened. Her companions were close. Soft weeping floated in the tight space, and guilt stabbed at her. Maybe she shouldn't have followed them. Maybe they wouldn't have been taken if she hadn't scared them into that alley. But then she shook her head. No. They were easy targets. These monsters would have spotted them and spooked them into some place where they could abduct them.

She hadn't made this worse. She had to believe that. She couldn't consider otherwise, couldn't let the guilt eat at her. It would keep her from thinking a way out of this. For all of them.

The weeping belonged to Pam. Apparently she

couldn't keep it together, even to keep her daughter calm.

Aimee's small voice pleaded, "Momma, Momma. What's wrong? Where are we going?"

Darby closed her eyes against her voice.

"Momma, I'm scared. Tell me, Momma. What's happening?"

Pam only cried harder. Darby crept across the floor, stretching out a hand until she touched someone's arm. She flexed her fingers, confirming that it was Pam. "C'mon, keep it together. We'll be okay as long as we stay calm." She didn't know whether that was true or not, but she knew falling apart wouldn't get them anywhere either.

The van slowed, bumping along an uneven surface. She tensed, waiting, turning her stare toward the double doors, waiting for them to open. For a brief second, she considered telling Pam and Aimee the true nature of what they were up against, but she didn't want to deal with hysterics.

The doors opened and they were hauled out with rough hands. Marcus walked ahead of the other three with loose, confident steps. She scanned their new surroundings. There was a house, large and sprawling. Snow-shrouded trees crowded the log and rock structure. It was the kind of place a tourist would want to rent. A lovely snowbound getaway. Smoke curled from its chimney invitingly like something on a postcard. She thought of the recent victims and wondered if this was where they had met their end.

They were no longer in town. From the thick press of forest around them that much was clear. But they hadn't been in the van that long. They couldn't be too far from town. She stared up into the sky. It was nearly dark.

Snow had started to fall again in fat flakes. She lowered her face away from the cold kiss, blinking as the flaky white collected on her lashes.

As they were led up the porch steps and inside the house, Darby stayed close to Pam and Aimee. The heat hit her, warming from the outside in.

"Ah, you've returned at last." A slender man who barely looked twenty unfolded himself from a sofa positioned before the great fire. He wore a thick black sweater and jeans. Clean-shaven, hair close-cropped, he looked collegiate. Not like a bloodthirsty beast of untold years.

Age was deceptive when it came to lycans. She knew this. Knew that if this was their alpha, he had to be older than the others. The most dangerous of them all.

His pewter gaze roved over each of them, lingering, assessing, before settling on her. "Ah, you've brought us something special it seems," he said in cultured tones, overenunciating his words.

He approached, appraising her carefully. That silver-eyed gaze made her want to squirm but she held her ground. "This is far finer than the usual fare you bring back. Good work, gentlemen." The alpha brushed a lock of hair back off her shoulder and she flinched.

"Yes. We got lucky, Cyprian. I find her interesting as well. This one might be worth keeping."

"The bitch did this to my face." The lycan—Marcus—she struck with the two-by-four motioned to his almost-healed wounds, clearly disagreeable to the suggestion of keeping her alive. "I don't want to keep her around."

Cyprian sighed and rolled his eyes. "Stop being such a child, Marcus. You're fine. And we're not exactly in a position to be choosy." He waved a hand around them. "Our numbers are dwindling here."

Cyprian's eyes narrowed as he studied her. "It has been some time since we've had a female in our pack."

"Yeah. They keep getting wiped out by—"

Cyprian moved then. His arm shot out in a blur she could hardly process. All she knew was that Marcus was standing one moment and across the room the next. If Darby had any doubt that Cyprian was the alpha, it was gone. "Silence! Don't speak his name. I told you, I don't want to hear."

Aimee started to cry in earnest. No more soft weeping. Even with her faced buried against her mother's leg, the wails came across loud and clear.

Darby patted the girl's back. Her mother seemed incapable, staring vacantly into space. It was like she was locked somewhere inside herself, unable to come out.

Cyprian turned a gracious smile on Darby. "Pardon me, you shouldn't have to see our squabbling. It's really quite rude of us. We obviously need a woman's touch to help tame our wild ways." He turned his attention on Aimee. "Don't cry, little one. This shall all be over soon." He patted the girl's head.

Pam didn't seem inclined to do anything except stare numbly into space. Darby pressed closer, hugging the child to her side.

"You. You're different." Cyprian wagged his finger at her, smiling as if she were a mischievous child who'd played a prank. "What is it about you, hm?"

Darby swallowed, knowing exactly what he meant, what he *sensed* about her, but not about to point out to him that he had a witch in his grasp. Especially since she didn't mean to be in his grasp for long.

Suddenly, his smile slipped. An intent look came over his face as he stepped nearer. He reached for her throat with thin, long fingers. She leaned back and swatted at his hand, but he ignored her, seizing her necklace. Somehow it had slipped out from beneath her sweater and lay exposed.

"Interesting," he mused, inspecting each of the three charms. "What do we have here? Milk and let me guess—holy water? And this third must be . . . salt." His pewter gaze drifted back to her face. Lycans weren't the only thing out there with certain aversions. Silver might repel them, but demons had their Achilles' heel, too. And from the look in his face she guessed he knew this. "What ordinary female wears charms like these?"

Darby held her breath, saying nothing.

"So what? What does that mean?" Marcus grumbled, motioning to her necklace.

"That she's not your typical human." Cyprian angled his head, his look growing thoughtful. "Can I even say human? Is a witch even human?"

She flinched, even though she already knew he'd figured her out. "Yes, I'm human."

He continued to look her over as if she were a grand prize dropped in his lap. "A white witch, too. Tell me, dear, what is your power?" He waggled his fingers in an imitation of someone casting a spell. "What's your magic?"

She shook her head. The last thing she wanted to do was admit her ability to see into the future.

"Ah, come now. I'm sure it's something quite useful. Especially if you've chosen to live here in this frozen scrap of earth. You're avoiding demons, are you not? Why else would you be here?"

She shook her head, marveling at his insights. "Who are you?"

"Ah, surprised at my knowledge?" He chuckled and moved several steps down into a sunken living area. "Well, I've been around for a good many years. I've run into your kind before. That lycans are here at all can be credited to witches. I should be thanking you."

"Don't," she bit out, glaring at him as he poured himself a healthy dose of brandy. "I'm not the witch responsible for creating you."

"Care for a drink?" he asked, all politeness, as if he were a host entertaining guests and not a predator hungry for human flesh.

"No, thanks."

He took a sip and narrowed his gaze on her again. "Now. Do yourself a favor and tell me what your particular talent happens to be, my lovely."

She pressed her lips into a hard line, her hand tightening where she clutched Aimee.

"Not talking then? Shame." He snapped his fingers at the lycan called Marcus. "Take her to the master suite and lock her in."

Marcus didn't disguise his displeasure. "We're not having her?"

"She's too valuable," Cyprian replied. "Sooner

or later, we'll learn of her gift . . . and how we might use it to benefit us."

Devon nodded, the motion not even bouncing one of his blond dreadlocks. "Good idea." His handsome faced smiled at her. "And I rather like her. Wouldn't mind keeping her around. She's got spirit. That's what we need."

"No," she shouted as she was dragged, kicking and flailing, from Aimee and Pam. "Please! Let them come with me. If you harm either of them, I'll never talk! Never tell you anything!"

Marcus's hand on her arm twisted cruelly. "Don't be stupid. We gotta eat. Count yourself lucky that you won't be the meal—"

"Wait." Cyprian's hard voice stopped Marcus.

The alpha moved toward the child, stroking the cloud of her brown hair. Aimee gazed up at him with unblinking eyes, wide as saucers, her little form frozen as if she sensed he was something else, something more than a man. Something worse.

"Cute girl. I can see how you're fond of her. You are, aren't you?" His lips twisted in a cunning smile.

Darby could utter nothing, only stare, beseeching him with her eyes.

After a long moment, Cyprian thrust the little girl toward Darby. "Very well. Take her. She's my gift to you. For now anyway. If you don't come around, she'll endure the same fate as her mother."

As Aimee was shoved into her arms, Darby looked in horror at Pam. She could do nothing. Nothing to save her. Not if she wanted to save Aimee.

At that moment something came over Pam. It was like the woman woke from a deep sleep. She jerked where she stood, tossing her too-long bangs back from her eyes. She looked around, searching with wild eyes for her daughter.

"Aimee!" she shouted, diving for the child. "Where are you taking her? Come back here!" She was instantly caught up in the arms of one their captors. She thrashed fiercely, her hair flying in every direction.

Aimee struggled in Darby's arms to reach her mother. "Momma! Momma!"

Cyprian glanced at the window. Holding Aimee tight, Darby followed his gaze, her chest tightening, clenching painfully at the muted blue light suffusing the air.

"Quickly," Cyprian declared, waving a hand at Darby and Aimee. "Take them. Go. Before it's too late."

"Wait, please, I beg you." Her gaze slid to Pam, shrieking and fighting with surprising strength. "She's her mother. Please let her come with us. I'll give you what you want."

"Oh, you will. I have no doubt. But we have to feed. There's no choice in that. As it is, we're only left with her and she's sadly thin. Hopefully, she's enough and we won't try to break into your bedroom." Eyeing Pam, he frowned. "Now, unless, you want to lose your life as well—and the girl's—you better get behind that locked door."

At that moment, Cyprian winced and bent himself at the waist as if he had a stomach cramp. When he straightened, his eyes were gleaming an even brighter pewter. "Go," he rasped, his voice thick and garbled from teeth that looked sharper, longer than a second ago.

There was no time for talking anymore, only time for survival.

With a pained gasp, she swung Aimee up into her arms. Devon led the way, showing no signs of transitioning yet. Her legs worked fast, desperate to remove the girl from danger. Pam's screams rang in her ears as she carried a sobbing Aimee into the bedchamber.

Devon stared at her intently. The brightness of his gaze chilled her to the bones. "Be sure to lock the door. We might try to get in. Whatever you do, don't unbolt this door until morning."

She squared her shoulders. "How do you know I won't keep us locked in here forever?"

"Because you'd starve. Also—" He flicked a glance to the hinges. "We can get some power tools in here and remove the door if need be. But you can bet that would seriously annoy Cyprian."

He shut the door then, the slam reverberating on the air, its solid steel sealing them in tight. She rushed to bolt it against them.

The room was dark, its one window boarded up tight. The door was no ordinary door. She ran a hand over its length, feeling its cold, solid strength.

Pam's screams could still be heard, but quieter now, muted. The fight had left her. Probably the moment her daughter left her sight.

Still holding Aimee in her arms, Darby flipped on the light switch. Light flooded the room, and she looked around. It was your standard room. Bed, dresser, a small connecting bathroom.

"Where's my momma?" Aimee whimpered against her neck, her breath a warm fan of air on her skin.

"Shhh, honey." Darby curled up on the bed with her, hugging her little body close. "Momma's . . . gone." Darby closed her eyes in a tight blink, miserable as she uttered the words. The guilt was there, a sharp pang in her chest. She felt responsible for all of this.

"When she's coming back?"

"I—I don't know." Cowardly, she supposed, but Darby couldn't say it. She couldn't declare that Pam wasn't coming back. Crazy or not, she still clung to hope—to the belief that there was a chance. To not hope was to quit.

A strange silence pervaded the room. Even Pam

had ceased to scream. Darby stroked Aimee's hair and rocked her to sleep as she waited, listening. She wished she couldn't listen, but she did. Her ears strained for the slightest sound.

And then it came. A long, low howl. So close, so very near that she thought it could have been in the room with them. Several howls joined in, and she knew it was too late.

They'd answered the moon's call and shifted. She closed her eyes as the anguished howls rippled through her.

Then the screams began. Different from before. These screams ripped the air, without volition. This wasn't Pam fighting for her daughter. This was anguish. Terror. This was death.

Darby fumbled a hand for the remote control on the nightstand and powered on the flat screen hanging from the wall. Clicking through channels, she found a cartoon and turned the volume up, hoping to drown out the sounds of what was happening in the other room. She crooned to Aimee and rocked her faster, hoping she still slept. As if they could outrun the reality of Aimee's mother dying so brutal a death in the next room.

Darby inhaled a shuddering breath. She doubted she would ever outrun this night. If she survived, it would stay with her all of her days.

TWELVE

They surrounded her, hideous creatures on every side. Darby sucked in a breath and ran, spotting a break through the thick press of bodies and bolting for it.

They followed, running after her at a loping pace, toying with her, letting her stay just ahead of them but within range. Without any real hope.

Still, she ran. She fought to live, struggling with Aimee's weight in her arms. Her legs burned, lifting high in the snow. She stumbled and fell into a soft drift, the girl still clutched in her arms.

They surrounded her. Their monstrous shapes towering, blocking out anything else as they leaned over her, jaws slavering, dripping the gore from their last kill . . . from Pam onto the snow-covered earth.

Darby woke with a scream trapped in her throat, her chest heaving with deep, pained breaths as the cry lodged itself inside her like a heavy stone. She swallowed, fighting to keep silent as the vision faded from her mind—but not memory.

She'd learned at an early age to hold back the screams, tired of waking her mother and then, later, her aunts. Sick of facing the worry in their eyes that her gift, her magic, was more than she could handle.

She blinked against the thin blue light of the room. The television still blared loudly, an infomercial. She patted the bed around her, searching for the remote control.

Darby found it and punched the mute button, killing the sound. She listened. No sounds reached them from outside the room. The carnage, evidently, was over.

Aimee was curled against her. She never woke. Amid it all, she had slept and Darby suspected this was God's gift so she could cope. Darby clicked the television off, instantly drowning them in darkness. The only light came from the bedside clock on the dresser, its red numbers glowing 3:45.

She unwrapped herself from around Aimee, careful not to wake her as she slid off the bed. With silent steps, she approached the door and pressed her ear against it. Nothing. No more screaming. No more growling or howls or crashing furniture. They were gone. Or passed out. Or maybe they'd gone hunting for other victims. Either way, this could be her only chance—hers and Aimee's. They had to get away.

The fact that they had to escape beneath the lycans' very noses, creep past sleeping monsters—that one misstep and she and Aimee were both lost, dead—didn't change her mind. It was now or never. They might see the value in keeping Darby around, but Aimee would never be safe. It was only a matter of time before they went after the girl. Even with a fresh vision hanging over her head, a terrible harbinger she couldn't quite shake free from her thoughts, she knew she had to take a chance and run for it.

Suddenly a surge of warmth pervaded the room. An unnatural warmth. Like an oven door had been opened and a wave of roasting heat swept free. *Shit*!

Darby whirled around, her hands clenching into fists, looking, searching, knowing what she would find.

Not now.

But of course, it would happen now. Now when she was her most vulnerable. Now when she most needed help. That's always when a demon chose to call.

A great shadow slipped beneath the door and crawled along the floor and walls until materializing before her.

She had to tip back her head to meet its dead-eyed stare. This one was a beauty. The head of a serpent but the body of a battle-hardened gladiator. He leaned down toward her, his flicking tongue almost touching her nose.

She braced herself, legs squared.

"Shouldn't you be somewhere else?" she demanded, forcing a show of bravado. This demon frightened her more than those lycans outside this room. Lycans could kill her, but this demon could own her soul for eternity.

"There's been a lot of activity in this area. You're too hard to resist. Despite the abominable weather, I had to check you out for myself . . ."

So her visions hadn't gone undetected, after all. She was a fool to think otherwise. She knew how it worked. The same way it always had. Her visions attracted demons. Especially sucky since she couldn't control her visions. She had long accepted that—why else was she living all alone here? She might not be able to control her visions, but she could control her environment. Relocating to an environment abhorrent to demons was the responsible thing to do. It beat following in her mother's footsteps and taking her own life.

"That was unnecessary," she said.

The demon's slit eyes surveyed the room, his flat nostrils flaring wide as he lifted his face and scented the area. "Ah, lycans. You're in a bit of trouble. Couldn't you use some assistance?"

"No. Get out of here. I don't need or want anything from you." Instantly, her mind drifted back to the vision of her and Aimee running through the snow, lycans surrounding them. If it held true, she'd soon need serious assistance.

She shook the thought aside and reminded herself that she'd managed to beat out her visions before. Knowledge was power. Her visions could be averted. She'd simply make sure she didn't take off on foot through the wilderness with Aimee. Because she knew what would happen if she did.

"No? Not yet. You sure? Maybe I'll stick around until you do . . ." At that moment the demon shuddered, fading back to shadow for a moment before managing to regain form.

Darby smiled, knowing he was weakening in this cold. He wasn't going to stick around much longer. He couldn't. "I don't think you're staying." She chafed her hands over her arms. "*Brrr.* My, my, isn't it cold in here? You'd think they could adjust the thermostat. I think it's as cold in here as it is out there," she taunted.

As if her words did the trick, the demon shuddered like rippling water before her eyes. "I'll find you again."

"I don't think so." She'd managed to stave off visions for the most part these last few years. Once she managed to escape this nightmare, she'd move

north again. Another town. Another lonely existence. But *safe*—she'd have safety again.

With fresh determination feeding her heart,
Darby quickly moved to the bed. Looping her
arms beneath Aimee, she held her close, inhaling
and savoring the child's sweet scent for a moment.
When she turned back around the demon was
gone—not even its shadow lingered.

They had to slip out now. The lycans would
expect them to stay put—they wouldn't suspect
that she'd dare come out while they were in full
shift. She pressed her ear close to the door again,
listening for several moments. Her adrenaline
rushed, pounding in her veins. Readjusting Aimee
in her arms, she carefully unlocked the door, mentally ordering her hands to stop shaking so much.

She stood still for a moment with the door
unlocked. She waited, in case they'd heard the
faint click, as though she expected the lycans
to burst through the unlocked door and pounce
upon her.

Nothing. The silence hung as thick as the odor
of death on the air. Tightening her single arm
around Aimee, she turned the knob and opened
the door. She scanned the hall before stepping out,
grateful for the runner that deadened her steps.

She moved along the long corridor, easing on
silent feet, hardly breathing, praying Aimee made

no sounds and that she didn't see her mother's corpse.

The coppery scent of blood hit her before she even entered the main living area. Two lycans lay sprawled within the gory mess, their grotesque forms sated, blood glistening crimson on their gray and brown fur. She swallowed back a cry at the remains of Aimee's mother flung about the room. There wasn't much left of her. Hardly anything to tell that she had even been a person.

Forcing down the surge of bile that rose in her throat, Darby made her way carefully past the sleeping forms, her eyes darting everywhere, searching for a glimpse of car keys, all the while wondering: *Where were the other three?* Hopefully they were long gone from here, out for a midnight run or wreaking damage elsewhere.

Still, no sight of the keys. Would they have left them in the vehicle? Did they put them away somewhere?

She opened the front door without a sound. Still, she cast a glance over her shoulder, assuring herself the two lycans slept. Slipping outside, she hoped they didn't feel the cold she let inside and awake. Once on the porch, she picked up her pace. She went for the car first. It would be easier to maneuver than the van.

Please be in the car, please be in the car.

If the keys weren't there, they would have to hike it out on foot. At night, in this weather, God knows how they would manage. And then it occurred to her that would be just like in her vision. She couldn't do that. No matter what, she couldn't let it come to that.

Crouching beside the car, she spied the keys through the window. With a sharp exhale, she awkwardly opened the back door and secured Aimee on the soft leather of the backseat, buckling her at the waist and letting her slump to the side. As quietly as possible, she shut the car door and got behind the wheel. As she turned the ignition, the car rumbled to life with a quiet purr.

Yes.

Immediately, her eyes flew to the rearview mirror, expecting the sleeping lycans to pour outside after her, but nothing happened as she put the car in drive and rolled away. The road was clearly marked and she followed the path through the trees. Her breathing eased and elation filled her as she put more distance between them and the house.

The narrow road finally ended and they came to a two-lane country road. She hesitated, looking left and right, trying to gauge which one led back to town, wishing she knew the area better.

She turned right, detecting a faint pink tinge to

the night sky in that direction and assuming it was the lights from town.

She pushed harder on the accelerator, anxious to reach town and people, safety from the beasts that prowled the moon-soaked night. The image of Niklas filled her mind then. She didn't know why she thought of him just then except that she suspected he knew about these lycans—that he was here because of them. *And that he'd kissed you and touched you and made you feel alive in a way that you haven't felt in years. Maybe ever.*

She shook her head. It didn't mean anything. She wouldn't find him waiting for her. So he'd fixed her window and replaced her heater. That didn't mean anything. Those were just actions of a nice guy who felt sorry for her.

She followed the curve of the road, her hands clenched tightly on the steering wheel, excited in the knowledge that she'd escaped. That her vision hadn't come to pass.

A shape suddenly jumped in the middle of the road. She cried out as the headlights briefly lit upon the bearlike creature. She swerved to avoid hitting the beast, even knowing it was no bear. She tried to right the vehicle but it was too late. She drove off the road, crashing into a large drift of snow with a jarring thud. Snow slapped against the windshield in a heavy deluge.

Her breath exploded in loud pants from her lips. The car still sputtered with life. She put it in reverse and pressed on the pedal. The tires spun, snow spitting up and covering the windows. They weren't going anywhere. The car was buried.

She took several even breaths and peeled her fingers free from the steering wheel.

She couldn't see anything. Snow covered almost all the windows, except the back windshield. She looked through the rearview mirror. No movement. Nothing but a world of white. She tried to back out again even though she knew it was useless. The engine revved pathetically. They weren't going anywhere.

She looked over her shoulder. Aimee was awake, peering at her with wide, uncertain eyes. The sight made her chest tighten almost painfully.

"Where's Momma?" she whispered, her small, colorless lips barely moving.

Darby undid her seat belt and climbed into the back with her. Avoiding the question, she said, "I'm going to help you, Aimee. Do you believe me?"

The girl nodded, but repeated her question. "Where's Momma?"

Darby glanced out the windows, looking for any sign of the lycan she'd seen on the road, the one that made them crash. She hadn't forgotten about him.

"Remember those bad men?" She flicked her gaze down to Aimee for half a second before looking out the back window again, scanning for movement, knowing they weren't alone.

"Yes."

She sucked in a deep breath, knowing Aimee wasn't going to trust her if she started out lying to her. She locked gazes with her again. "They took your momma, honey. She's gone." She waited a moment for this painful information to sink in. Aimee stared at her with wide, uncomprehending eyes. "But we aren't going to let them take us, okay? You got that?"

"They took Momma?" Her lips quivered. Her small body started to collapse. "I want them to give her back. Tell them to give her back."

Darby shook her gently and then pulled her into a firm embrace, rubbing her back with quick, firm circles. "I know, I know. But they're not going to do that. They're bad men." *Monsters.* "Your momma wanted you to be safe. And I'm going to see that you are."

A long mournful howl floated on the air. Darby quickly weighed their options. Wait here, a sitting duck, or attempt to reach town on foot. Another howl floated on the air, and her decision was made.

It didn't have to go down as in the vision. She could still avert that fate. A desperate fury rose up inside her. What would be the point of having these visions, if she couldn't reverse them?

At the moment nothing moved outside. Everything was still.

She quickly adjusted the zipper on Aimee's coat, pulling it as high as it could go. As if that would be enough to ward off the beasts hunting them. Darby pulled the hoods of their coats over their heads and smiled tremulously at the child. She took Aimee's hand and gave it a tight squeeze. Holding the little fingers tightly in her own, she swung open the back door and stepped out.

THIRTEEN

C'mon, baby." Darby forced a cheerful ring into her voice as her boots sank down into the snow. "We're going to have to walk the rest of the way into town, but once we get there, I'm going to make you the biggest ice cream sundae you've ever seen."

"What about that chocolate cake?"

"Ahh, that sounds even better, doesn't it? Excellent suggestion. We'll have warm chocolate cake with ice cream on the side. How does that sound?"

With a sniff and swipe at her nose, Aimee nodded, her small hand snug within Darby's. "Maybe Momma will get away and meet us there? She likes cake, too."

Darby's heart clenched. She couldn't bring herself to answer the girl—to tell her that her momma was never going to get away. Not yet. Not until they were out of this.

The cold cut into them like knives as they moved. Darby wrapped an arm tightly around

Aimee's shoulders and walked quickly, pulling her close. She bent her head and tucked her chin into her parka as they advanced down the road.

After a moment, she glanced behind her, satisfied to see that the car was out of sight. They were making good ground at least. She opened her mouth to offer an assurance that they would be there soon, when another howl ripped the night. So close it felt like the animal was on top of them.

She froze, looking wildly all around her, expecting to see a lycan bounding out of the trees at them. She saw nothing, but in the distance, she heard a thrashing sound, like something tearing through the brush.

"Run," she gasped, pulling Aimee along. Just as in her vision, she ran, her feet pumping hard through the snow, the moisture soaking her jeans up to the knees.

Aimee tripped and Darby swung her up into her arms. Heedless of the extra weight, she ran, her legs burning from the strain. Her lungs ached, ready to explode from her chest.

The thrashing sounds intensified, were all around them now. She saw it then, a flash of eyes through the trees along the road. Icy silver and surrounded by the blackest of fur. They trailed her, toying with her.

The howls congested the air now. The forest

was alive with the sounds of them—predators. The beating of their feet. The harsh crash of their breaths. Just as in her vision.

She swallowed thickly and stopped, dropping against a tree along the roadside. The snow-covered bark chafed her back. Aimee's warm breath fanned her throat, a bittersweet reminder of why she had to live. Her survival was for both of them. Aimee didn't lift her head, didn't look, didn't speak. Her thin arms clung so tightly Darby could scarcely draw breath.

She held herself still—quiet—her gaze darting around, plotting her next move, wondering if they should just find a spot and hide until daybreak.

Too late—the lycans emerged from the trees, all five of them. Apparently the two in the house had woken. They were varying shades of brown, gray and black. All bloodstained and grisly. Enormous, with slavering teeth that dripped gore from their recent kill. She wanted to look away but dared not.

They crossed the road in a slow, stalking pace, fanning out in a wide semicircle before her. Their great hulking shapes were covered in matted fur. But even the fur did not hide the sinew rippling beneath.

"Hey, remember me?" Darby fumbled for her necklace, holding it out by the chain, letting the charms dangle. "You wanted to keep me around, remember? I'm useful."

At the sound of her voice, Aimee started to lift her head to investigate. Darby pushed it back down ungently.

She scanned the five creatures, trying to gauge which one was the alpha, Cyprian—the one she knew to direct her plea to. For some reason, her attention centered on the black-furred one. Not the largest, but the others seemed to walk in his shadow. He led the pack and stopped a few feet in front of Darby.

She dangled the necklace, her voice a terrible quiver and reed thin on the air. "Remember me? You want to keep me around."

The lycan's great jaws peeled back to reveal his yellow-stained teeth. Faint rivulets of pink, diluted blood traced his teeth and lined his gums. He released a low growl.

Running would be useless. For one fleeting moment, she considered doing that ultimate thing—the one thing she vowed never to do. *Summoning a demon to aid her.*

The question she asked herself was what she valued more—her soul or her life? Which was she willing to sacrifice? She knew that answer. She'd always known that answer.

With conviction burning in her heart, she

pressed her lips tightly together, silencing herself should she feel tempted to utter the words, to shout out for a demon's aid in a moment of pain or distress.

The alpha stretched his neck so that his face was close . . . close enough that she smelled the sourness of his breath, felt the heat of it fanning her face. She squeezed her eyes shut and turned her face, waiting, hoping it wouldn't hurt, hoping he ended it quickly, that there would be no suffering—especially for Aimee.

The pain never came.

A shot exploded on the air. And then another.

Darby's eyes flung wide open. The black-furred lycan no longer stood before her. He was gone. A blurry ink spot on the white landscape.

She whipped her gaze around and spotted a man holding a weapon. He was armed to the teeth, ammo strapped to his chest, and a gun in each hand. A knife glinted from a sheath at his waist and he wore multiple holsters. He was armed for battle. For lycans.

Her gaze took all this in with a sweep—before actually seeing him. The real him. The face of the man she knew. Niklas. Her heart leapt with instant hope. And something else strange and indefinable. He stood tall and capable-looking, his indigo eyes glowing with that otherworldly light, and something besides her heart leapt. Her stomach flipped.

Two lycans lay dead. Blood so thick that it looked black seeped into the snow around their bodies.

She watched Niklas approach and riddle several more bullets into each of the bodies. Steam wafted over the wounds. Silver. It had to be. She knew it was the only thing that could stop a lycan.

A blur flashed across the air. In a blink, Niklas turned to greet the new threat. They came together simultaneously in a crash of bone on bone.

Niklas had been lucky with the shots. She was sure his luck wouldn't last. Not against creatures with supernatural powers. Even if he beat this one, there were still two other lycans unaccounted for. Her skin shivered at the memory of them. She wasn't sticking around for them to direct their attention back on her and Aimee.

She lowered Aimee to the ground and grabbed hold of her hand. "C'mon, sweetie. Keep up." Holding tightly, she took off, pulling the child after her.

Even as they tromped through the snow, guilt pained her for leaving Niklas. She wanted to stay—wanted to help him. But she knew she could do nothing except get them both killed if she did that. And there was Aimee she had to consider.

"Were those monsters?" Aimee gasped beside her, and Darby grimaced, realizing she'd let the girl see them, after all. Guess she could only shield her from so much when this was the frightening reality that surrounded them.

Ignoring the question, she tugged harder on her slight hand. "C'mon, keep up. We're putting them behind us."

Then suddenly she wasn't holding anything anymore. Her fingers groped air. She spun around—assuming the child had fallen—ready to haul the girl back to her feet again.

But she was gone. Darby jerked her gaze off the empty space in front of her, where she expected Aimee to be, and scanned the area all around her.

From the corner of her eye she glimpsed a streak of brown. She narrowed her gaze on the spot and a lycan running away through the trees with Aimee struggling in his arms.

"Aimee!" she screamed, running several steps before tripping on a tree root hidden beneath the snow and falling to her knees. She was up again, still screaming even when she could no longer see them. They were gone.

She followed in the lycan's tracks, only dimly wondering about Cyprian and Niklas as she focused on finding Aimee. She struggled ahead, even after it became clear she wouldn't catch up with them. The only sound she could hear anymore was the crashing of her labored breath on the vanishing night. And then a scream—shrill enough to shatter glass.

She froze for a fraction of a moment, goose bumps breaking out over her flesh. "Aimee!"

Spurred to life, she pushed harder then, freezing tears trailing her cheeks as she ran.

She stopped suddenly, seeing something, the bright splash of pink that was Aimee's coat through the trees in the road ahead. She rushed forward, numb to her actions, uncaring that she in no way could stop this from happening. *She had to try.* Her aunts had been there for her after her mother died. Someone needed to be there for Aimee, too.

She grabbed the discarded coat with both hands and hugged it close, glancing around, despair rising up to choke her as she felt the slick sensation of blood on the fabric. "Aimee!" she screamed. "Aimee!"

A shot rang out in the woods, reverberating off the towering trees.

She picked up the tracks in the snow again and charged through the trees, stopping when she came upon a person bent in the snow.

Catching her balance, she eyed the broad back of the familiar figure. "Niklas?" she whispered. Apparently he was okay.

He unfolded his great length from where he crouched, turning to face her. And that's when she saw his arms weren't empty. He cradled an unconscious Aimee, and behind them lay the corpse of the lycan, gradually returning to his human form.

"Aimee," she breathed, reaching for the girl, eager to take her back into her arms. "You saved her."

He sharply pulled her out of Darby's reach, like a toy he would hoard for himself. "No. I was too late," he announced. "She's dead."

Darby's gaze flew to the still girl, only then seeing the nasty wound at her shoulder—the shredded purple sweater soaked in blood, where the lycan's teeth had torn through to get to her. A choked sob escaped her. *No! No! I promised she would be okay.*

Her small face was ashen, lips a pale purple tinge. She was still, hanging limply, lifelessly in Niklas's arms. *Dead*. Darby's shoulders slumped and a heaviness lodged deeply in her chest.

And then Aimee let out a little mewl of pain.

"Wait!" Darby cried, stretching her hands for her again. "You're wrong! She's alive!"

Relief surged in her heart, wild as the fluttering wings of a bird just released from its cage. With this relief mingled a hope so palpable she could taste it. Aimee was going to be okay. They were both going to be okay. She stretched her arms for the child again.

"No!" Niklas pulled Aimee out of the way, his features stark and relentless in the light of the moon. "She's bitten."

The reminder struck her like a physical blow. Her arms fell to her sides as she let this penetrate, sink in in all its horror . . .

Bitten by a lycan.

She shook her head as if she could erase his words. As if she could wipe free this terrible reality.

She stared hard into his unblinking gaze, searching as denial rose up inside her. "What are you saying?" she asked through numb lips, the relief disappearing inside her, changing to something painful and aching.

"I think you know." He cocked his head. "You know how this all works. What they are." He waved a hand, motioning to the dead lycan, now a human corpse in the snow. "You know what it means if you're bitten."

Darby nodded jerkily. "Yes. Yes, I do."

Jonah had been part of her life for a long time. Even though he was a hybrid lycan—a dovenatu— she knew all about lycans. The reason they even existed was that one of her kind had bought into a demon's empty promises and started the curse.

"I do know about these monsters," she admitted. For half a breath, she thought he flinched at her words. "But I also know you just have to kill the alpha—"

"The alpha that got away," he reminded her harshly.

A muscle along his cheek rippled with tension, and she guessed that this was a sore point for him. She caught his meaning. If he hadn't had to save her and Aimee, he would have killed the alpha. Accusation shone in his indigo gaze.

She squared her shoulders. "Then we have to find him."

"Yeah, that's kind of what I'm trying to do . . . what I *was* doing until I stopped to save your ass."

"Sorry to be such an inconvenience," she snapped.

He shook his head angrily and nodded down at Aimee. "We can't risk letting her—"

"No," she cut in, not about to let him say it. Not about to let him utter that they should kill the child rather than let her live out the month.

"She's dead," he uttered flatly. "You're not doing her any favors if you let her live through the month. Think of her."

"We're not killing her," she repeated.

"I'll do it. You don't have to be here—"

"Some favor! You think that will make it *better*?

Easier for me? It's not about *me* and what I can or can't handle. It's about her. She deserves someone to fight for her."

"Face facts, Darby. Ugly as they are, when the moon rises she's going to turn into one of them. A tiny monstrosity with a hunger for flesh."

She flinched but held her ground. Her whole life had been ugly facts. She was sick to death of existing under a dark cloud of ugly facts. Existing and not living. Enduring a reality that was not of her making and beyond her control. For once she wanted to take control, wanted to beat the odds. She wanted to win Aimee her life back. And maybe in doing that, she would win herself back, too. She'd no longer feel like a prisoner within her own life.

She stepped closer. Moistening her lips, she stared into Niklas's eyes and rested a hand on his arm. Even through the thick layer of sleeve, his heat reached her. That arm tightened, the muscles clenching beneath her fingers.

"Please," she whispered, beseeching him with her eyes. "We can try."

Aimee rustled in his arms and they both glanced down at her. The child looked angelic asleep and Darby didn't know how he could consider snuffing out her life . . . how he could *not* consider fighting for her.

She looked up at him and asked in a quiet voice, "Haven't you ever fought for anything? For anyone?"

"When there's no chance of winning? What would be the point?" His voice fell cold and empty, and she was convinced this was a man who had never loved.

Maybe who never could.

"*Hope* is the point." And love. She already loved this girl, and she wasn't ready to let her go.

He shook his head once. "You've no idea what we're risking. Keeping her alive until the next moon endangers innocent lives."

So pragmatic. Where was his heart? "I'm not going to let you do this," she bit out again, louder this time, reaching for Aimee, grasping the girl with both hands. "Give her to me."

"You can't win this."

"Look. We'll stay with you. We have a month to track this alpha. We'll find him. We'll kill him before the next full moon and she shifts. Then we can return her to her grandmother—where she was going with her mother in the first place."

"It won't be that simple."

Darby shook her head. "She's got a chance. We have to give her that chance." She inhaled bitter cold air into her lungs and added, "If it doesn't work out, I'll do it myself. When the time comes."

He stared at her for a long moment through narrowed eyes. Snow gathered in his lashes as he studied her. Then as if reaching a decision, he blinked and strode past her, still carrying Aimee. "Come on, it's cold. Let's get somewhere warm before we start tracking Cyprian again. I killed the others. There's just him now. He'll be desperate to increase his ranks. My guess is he'll move into a larger population and try to lose himself in the masses—make it harder for me to sniff him out."

She walked quickly after him, trying to keep up with his long strides, her heart surging inside her at his indirect agreement.

"You'll do as I say. Exactly what I say. Without question," he called over his shoulder. "Otherwise this ends now. Before it even begins."

"Of course," she agreed, panting to keep up, her boots crunching a steady rhythm over the snow. "How do you know so much about this Cyprian? Are you the one they mentioned? The one who's been hunting them?"

His lips twisted as he walked, carrying Aimee in his arms as if she were nothing more than a feather. "That would be me. I've managed to decimate his pack. He, however, still eludes me. The bastard has nine lives." They approached the Hummer parked alongside the road, not far from where she crashed the lycans' car. He opened the back door and carefully laid Aimee on the backseat.

Jonah had mentioned lycan hunters before to her, a large, secret organization called NODEAL. "Are you part of NODEAL?"

He slid her a look. "You know a lot about lycans. No, I'm not. I do things solo."

"Why are you after this particular pack? Did they do something to you?"

He motioned for her to get in the back beside Aimee. She slid in beside the girl but still looked up at him, waiting for an answer.

"They took my mother," he responded flatly and then shut the door in her face.

She felt his announcement like a slap. She knew what it was like to lose a mother. Her mother had been unable to handle her life as a witch . . . the constantly appearing demons trying to steal away her soul. It tormented her only further when Darby's gift ended up being something that had demons appearing all the time.

Getting struck with a vision at any odd time of the day became more than an inconvenience. It was dangerous when it tracked demons to her like a moth to flame—tracked them to her and her mother.

Her mother couldn't cope. Not with any of it—

but especially not with Darby. So she quit on all of it. She quit on herself and Darby. She quit on life.

Darby gawked at the back of Niklas's head as he got in the front and started the car.

"How long ago was that?" she asked.

He lifted one broad shoulder, his gaze catching hers in the rearview mirror. "Ten years."

"You've been hunting this pack for ten years?"

"Lycans haven't been around this long because they're stupid and easy to kill." Defensiveness edged his voice. "So, yeah. I've hunted Cyprian and his pack for ten years." His eyes hardened and she knew he was battling rage for having lost him. For having been so close only to come up empty-handed again. "I'll hunt him forever, if I have to."

She bit her lip and glanced down at the inert girl.

"And what about you?"

She tensed at his question, her thoughts still tangled up in the painful memory of her mother. "What about me?"

"How long you been hiding from demons in the Great White North?"

She jerked from the question. *How did he know she was a witch?*

As if reading her mind, he answered, "I saw your necklace . . . and the way you act . . . It wasn't hard to put together. Not if you know witches are out there."

Darby stammered as he put the car in drive and headed into town. She wondered how he even knew witches existed. Most people didn't know. As far as she knew, even lycans and NODEAL hunters knew little of them. At least not about true witches: white witches and demon witches. Her kind kept a low profile, obviously preferring to stay off the radar. The world didn't know about them.

But he did. He knew her secret. She bit her lip, wondering how many other surprises he had in store for her.

FOURTEEN

They drove directly to Darby's apartment. She followed Niklas up the stairs and inside as he carried Aimee and placed her on the bed. She got to work cleaning Aimee's wound and bandaging it up. She changed her into the smallest T-shirt she owned, guessing they wouldn't be able to claim her luggage from the bus station.

"We're going to have to get her some new clothes."

He nodded. "I'm going to get the rest of my things from my room. I need to gather some other supplies, too, so I'll see what I can find for her. I'll be back in a few hours. We don't want Cyprian to get too much of a head start."

She walked him to the door, rubbing her hands up and down her arms and telling herself that she just hadn't warmed up yet. Even though—for once—her apartment was cozy and warm. The cold clung. A bone-deep cold that she doubted she'd ever be free from—especially after tonight.

Tonight she'd shed her last scrap of hope that she could ever be safe. Ever be free of all the ugly things that walked this earth alongside the good and innocent.

She was done hiding. It was time to fight.

"How do you know where to go . . . where Cyprian will go next?"

At the door, he paused and turned to face her. "It's time we're up front about a few things that we've been skirting around."

She nodded, but her throat felt suddenly tight, her skin itchy beneath his regard. "You know what I am." They'd covered that already.

"Yeah."

She crossed her arms over her chest. "How do you know about witches?" They hadn't covered that and it was still nagging her how he knew about her kind.

"My mother."

She angled her head. "She told you?"

"No." He looked away from her then, stared somewhere over her shoulder as if he saw something there, something being played out just for his eyes alone. "She was one. Like you—a witch."

Her heart leapt, unaccountably excited to discover they had this connection. "Your mother was a white witch?"

"At first. A white witch. And then she sold her soul."

Darby pulled back as if physically struck. It was her worst nightmare. Her mother had killed herself rather than enslave herself to a demon. As much as she struggled with her mother's suicide, it would have been so much worse to lose her to a demon. "Your mother contracted with a demon?"

He looked back at her then, faced her with his indigo eyes flat and void of emotion—as if this information affected him not at all. "She gave up her soul and turned herself over to a demon."

"Why would she do such a thing?"

"She did it for me. In exchange for my soul."

Darby looked him up and down, as if he wore his soul on the outside and she could see it before her. "What do you mean? How was your soul in danger?"

"I was infected by a lycan. When I was sixteen Cyprian and his pack attacked me and some friends. I escaped, but it was too late. I was infected just like that girl in there and on my way to becoming a . . . *monster*—I think that's what you called it."

She nodded, remembering that she'd said that. And he'd flinched. Why? He stood before her, obviously not one of them. His mother's sacrifice had worked and saved him. So then, why—

"My mother did the only thing she could think of. She exchanged her soul for mine."

"So a demon lifted your curse and took her instead." Darby inhaled, unable to imagine how that must have made him feel. How it still made him feel, knowing that his mother sacrificed herself for him. "That must have been awful for you."

He didn't disagree. Or agree. His lips twisted in a nasty smile. "My mother should have perhaps had more care with her words."

A sinking sensation filled her stomach, but she waited, dreading, knowing there was more . . . worse to come.

"She asked for my soul . . . but she didn't ask that I return to the way I was before." He chuckled humorlessly. "Damn demons. They're clever fuckers. Never can trust them."

A fist tightened around her heart. She was almost afraid to ask, but she couldn't *not* know.

"What happened to you?" Because whatever happened to him was evidently what shaped him into what he *was* now. Who was this man standing before her? It would be a good idea to know who she was dealing with, especially considering she'd just teamed up with him for the next month.

His gaze drilled into her, as relentless as steel. It didn't occur to her that she should possibly not trust him. He'd done nothing but come to her aid from the start . . . despite the danger that seemed to drip off him.

"I'm a lycan."

This pronouncement dropped like a stone through the air—falling with a heavy *thunk* in her knotted-up stomach. She resisted the urge to take an instinctive step back.

Then it occurred to her that this wasn't possible. She'd seen him on multiple nights when the moon was full. He was no monstrous furred beast.

She laughed then, the sound nervous and tinny, still unconvinced. "No, you're not."

"It's true. I'm a lycan, just one with a soul." He uttered this admission quietly, evenly and without feeling. Which had to be an act. How could you be a lycan and not have any emotion over that fact?

Her breath expelled in a rush. "How is that possible? What does that even mean? A lycan with a soul?" She shook her head, pressing her fingertips to her suddenly aching temples. It dawned on her that she hadn't slept—not really, not peacefully, in over twenty-four hours.

"It means I have free will. I possess a soul, so I possess the choice to do right or wrong . . . like every other human. I don't have to shift."

"But you can."

He hesitated, as if he wanted to deny it. "Yes."

She nodded. Okay. A lycan with free will. With

a soul. That didn't sound so bad. "Except you're not a human."

"Yeah. That's the catch."

"You sound a lot like a hybrid."

"A dovenatu?" He looked at her sharply. "You know about them?"

She nodded. "I was friends with one." Two, she guessed, thinking about Sorcha, Jonah's wife.

"There's not that much difference between us, I guess. We both possess free will. Except that I seem to be aging at a normal rate, like a human. And I don't know how it was for your friend, but it's a real struggle every full moon to resist the shift." He dragged a hand through his hair. "Hell, I don't know. I guess I'm more lycan than human."

She stepped closer, touching his arm lightly. "You're not like them. Not at all. You're . . ." *You're good.* She swallowed, an surge of emotion welling up inside her. "You saved us. You helped me the other night." She motioned a hand to her window. "For God's sake, you fixed my window."

He laughed that low rumble again that did things to her insides. "Yeah, well, sometimes it's hard to believe that I'm anything but a monster when every moonrise my body burns to shift into one of them."

"And have you? Have you ever broken down and done that?"

"Not in years. In the beginning, I couldn't fight it. I've mastered control over it since then. I won't ever transition again."

"When you did . . . those years ago when you lost it . . ." She had to hear him say he didn't hurt someone, that he didn't do what *they* did. She had to know she and Aimee would be safe around him.

His eyes fastened on her. "I held on to myself, if that's what you're asking. I never deliberately harmed anyone. Apparently when the demon granted my mother's wish for me to keep my soul, he took away the lycan's hunger for flesh."

She released a breath she didn't know she'd been holding. "That's how you track Cyprian then. Using your lycan instincts?"

"We're connected." He nodded. "That's how we'll find him. The end is finally near. There's only him now. He doesn't have anyone left to hide behind."

They stood silent for a long moment, each studying the other with all walls removed, barriers knocked down. He knew what she was and now she knew the full story about him.

As different as they were, she realized they were alike. Two people—or whatever they were—isolated by their very nature. Darby could relate to him.

The air suddenly altered, became something thick, tension swirling around them so dense she could swim in it. Her throat constricted and she fought to swallow. In that moment, if she had wanted to speak she couldn't have.

His gaze dropped to her hand on his arm, still resting there. Everything flooded back to her then. Everything. Their kiss, long and deep and smoldering. His heat, his taste. Her need and hunger for more of him. For all of him.

She'd thought he'd growled during that kiss, and now she guessed that he probably had. And still that didn't bother her. A tremor of excitement raced up her spine.

His gaze slid up from her hand on his arm then. She fell into his gaze. That twisting flame of light was back in his indigo eyes. "You might not want to do that," he rasped.

"What?"

"Touch me."

"Oh." Her hand slipped from his arm. She rubbed her fingertips together at her sides. They felt bereft, cold on the air.

"I didn't open up to you and tell you about myself because I wanted your pity or soft looks. I especially wasn't trying to get you to pet me like I'm some sort of puppy—"

"I wasn't doing that," she said hotly, scanning his six-feet-plus hard body. The last thing he reminded her of was a puppy.

"I told you the truth about me, about my mother, because you deserve to know. If we're in this together for the next month, then you should know all the factors."

His eyes were so cold, fathomless deep and impossible to read. The light inside them had vanished.

He spoke with such practicality. Like they were entering into some kind of business arrangement. There was nothing sentimental or friendly about his words. As much as she'd held herself from the world, something told her Niklas was an even harder case.

Not too comforting to consider, when she and Aimee would be in close quarters with him for the next month.

But they wouldn't *be* with him, she reminded herself. Not really. This was strictly a mission with no emotion involved. He wasn't invested like she was in saving Aimee's life. A fact she should remember so she didn't make any more overtures of friendship and embarrass herself by touching him again—by wanting and *craving* to touch him again. Another motive drove him and it had nothing to do with her. This was about his mother. About him.

"I appreciate you telling me everything." She nodded, trying to look unaffected, as cool and remote as he was. "You're right. We're in this together."

She still couldn't quite wrap her head around it all. She wondered about his mother. Thoughts of her must plague him, haunt him every day. She shivered at the thought of what he must endure, the agony of living with the knowledge that his mother sacrificed her life—her very soul—for him.

As much as the memory of her mother's death haunted her, Darby at least knew she was dead. He didn't have that peace. Was his mother even still a demon witch? Or was she dead now? Her soul forever lost for consorting with a demon?

Once a white witch entered into contract with a demon, she gained immortality. She lived forever at the mercy of her demon's whims.

Had his mother's demon somehow managed to bring about her death? Because that's what they did—tricky bastards. There was only one way a demon witch could be killed. Decapitation. Take the head and the demon was free to roam the earth in corporeal form. What every demon wanted. That was their ultimate goal.

He still watched her with his cold gaze, and she guessed he had good reason to be so cool and aloof. What happened to him could break anyone.

A small, mewling sound carried from the other room.

Niklas nodded in that direction. "The child. She's begun the transition."

"Her name is Aimee," she said. He could at least call her something besides *the child*.

He stared right through her like she hadn't said anything. "You may want to go to her. She'll be very uncomfortable. At least until it ends and she wakes."

Darby looked over her shoulder, peering into her dimly lit room. "What can I do to help her through it?"

"The fever will rage—no stopping that. Try to get her to drink. There's not much else you can do for her. It is what it is. Her human DNA is dying, turning over. She'll sleep for the next few days."

"A few days?" She blinked. "That's unnatural."

"She's an unnatural creature now." He cocked his head and gave her a look that reminded her that she was unnatural, too. Just as he was.

"We should cover as much ground as we can during the time she sleeps," he said brusquely. "It's going to be hard enough to track him, but when she wakes, she'll slow us down. I'll be back soon. Until then, try to get some rest yourself."

Rest. She doubted she could ever close her eyes again.

He opened the door and the muted light of day-break spilled through the door, a milky violet that promised sunlight to come later.

How she'd longed for the sight of that—every breath from this hellish night, she had prayed to make it to this moment, to see daylight one more time.

"There's something I have to know."

He cocked his head, waiting for her to elaborate.

"If you're not afflicted with a lycan's desire to feed, why not shift then? I mean . . . could it help? Could you track Cyprian quicker?"

He shut the door and faced her, crossing his arms over his chest and looking at her *that* way again. That intense and unnerving way that made her want to hide from his gaze.

She resisted stepping back and held her ground. She continued, babbling, "If you have free will, why won't you turn? It could give you an advantage, it could help—"

"It makes me too much like them."

She blinked once and stared at him hard. "But you're not. At least in the way that matters." But if he could be like them in other ways—tracking, speed, strength—he might be able to find them faster. "If it could help us . . ."

Her voice faded. His eyes gleamed down at her,

the light there bright and dangerous. He seemed untouchable. As beautiful as a fatal serpent. "All you need to know is that we do this my way."

Indignation flared hotly in her chest. It was her turn to cross her arms. "As far as explanations go, that's not good enough. You're going to have to do better than that."

His expression darkened, and she felt certain he'd had enough of *her*.

Bracing herself, she waited for what he would do next.

NIKLAS INHALED DEEPLY, NOT sure why he should explain anything to her at all. He didn't owe her anything.

Then why are you here? Why are you doing any of this at all?

Ignoring the nagging voice in his head that warned him he was getting too involved, he moved into her small apartment and lowered himself to the couch. After a moment, she moved to sit beside him.

"I finally pulled myself together about a year after I was turned," he began. "That's when I started hunting Cyprian's pack. I wasn't very good at first—the scent of any lycan would distract me and confuse me as to what trail I needed to follow. I was basically hunting them all. One night I came across a pair of lycans attacking a woman, a girl really." He winced. "Not much older than me."

His shoulders tensed, tightening as he saw the scene all over again in his head.

"What happened?"

"I engaged the lycans." His voice became clipped, emotionless, like he was reading off a piece of paper and not relating anything significant, but he would never forget the ugliness he had stumbled upon . . . what they were doing to that girl. "I tried to stop them, but they were strong." His jaw clenched. He told himself to relax, to not let the past affect him anymore. Easier said than done, he was discovering. He'd never told this story to another soul. *You never had anyone to tell it to before.*

He drew a deep breath through his nose, pushing that thought away. Being alone had never bothered him before. Meeting her shouldn't change that; it shouldn't bother him now. "As I said, I was new to it all. Inexperienced." He lifted one shoulder in a shrug. "I couldn't handle them on my own, in human form. I thought I needed an advantage. So I shifted."

"Did you beat them?" She winced at the question, clearly realizing he must have or he wouldn't be sitting in front of her.

He nodded. "I did. And the girl . . ." He stopped,

seeing the wide, haunted eyes, the blood soaking blond hair, staining it a deep brown.

Darby leaned forward anxiously. "Was she okay?"

He nodded again. "She was still alive, by some miracle." Then his words came quickly. "I approached her to try and help her and she just . . . screamed. And kept on screaming." Even now, he could hear the awful sound ringing in his ears, ripping through him.

Darby shook her head, a heaviness settling in her chest. "After you'd just saved her life?"

"I tried to talk to her, calm her down, but she wouldn't stop screaming. She took off running. She left the park and ran right out into the street." He paused, taking a breath. "A truck hit her. She died instantly."

Darby blinked. "You can't blame yourself for that. She was hysterical, traumatized from what they did to her."

"She ran into that street because of me." Because of the monster he was. "I should have left her alone." He shook his head. "No—I should never have shifted."

She placed her hand on his knee. Sensation zipped through him at the touch of her hand. He tensed beneath her fingers. She must have felt his tension, for she looked down to where she touched him. With a small gasp, barely audible, she snatched her hand away and buried it in her lap. Color flooded her cheeks, almost the same red as her hair, and he marveled at that. Women actually still blushed these days? Modesty and reticence had long since been absent from his life.

She moistened her lips and he followed the quick darting of her tongue, desire twisting in his belly. The air around them altered, became thicker, heavy with an aching awareness of each other.

"She ran into the street because of the lycans who attacked her. Not you."

He tore his gaze away from her mouth. "Don't you get it? It didn't matter. I looked like them. To her, I was one of them."

"Looking like them doesn't mean you're like them."

"That was the last time I ever shifted. I don't need to shift in order to beat them."

Something passed over her face.

"What?" he demanded.

"Maybe you do . . . I mean, you needed to do it then to overpower them, and you've been hunting Cyprian for a long time. Maybe you would have found them sooner if you weren't so hung up on shifting."

Her words struck a nerve. "It's the way it has to

be," he growled. "I won't risk shifting again, losing control—"

"You never lost control—"

"Drop it," he bit out, rising to his feet and moving toward the door again. "You mistake yourself if you think your opinion matters enough to change my mind on this."

That did the trick. She flinched, staring at him with hurt eyes. "I'm trying to help."

"You can help by following my lead on this." He drew a ragged breath and wondered why the way those hazel eyes stared at him affected him so much. Why she should affect him? "And stop asking me so many fucking questions."

Niklas left without another word and Darby locked the door behind him, noticing that her hands shook. Moving into her small bedroom, she checked on Aimee before stripping out of her clothes and stepping into the shower.

She arched her throat and let the warm water beat down on her body, luxuriating in the wet heat, letting it ease her sore muscles, thankful for being alive.

She envisioned Niklas as he had been tonight, fierce and wild fighting the lycans intent on devouring her, then almost tender as he told her about his past, revealing pieces of himself she felt sure he'd never shared with another soul. Until he shut her down, spoke to her so harshly at the end.

Except she couldn't forget his eyes.

Her hand brushed her breast and with some surprise she felt her nipple pebble-hard, aroused and sensitive. She released a moan and ducked her head under the spray of water, perfectly aware of the reason why her body was in such a state.

It had been a long time since she'd even been close to a man as sexy as Niklas. His body, his voice, everything about him aroused her.

She wanted him—no, she craved him. She ached just thinking about him. It took all her willpower not to fling herself at him.

The problem was that kiss. Maybe if she had never kissed him, she wouldn't be so convinced at how good they would be together—how amazing it would be.

She sighed. It was going to be a long month. Especially considering he looked at her as if she were an unwanted child foisted upon him that he must babysit. He was all hard resolve. There would be no repeat kisses.

When this was all over and she reentered the land of the living, the first thing she needed to do was get herself a boyfriend to satisfy the itch that Niklas had roused in her.

Who says you need a boyfriend to do that? Who

says you can't push Niklas into relieving that itch himself? You have a month . . .

A wicked smile curved her mouth at such bold and totally uncharacteristic thinking. She wasn't one to be aggressive—a lifetime of staying below the radar and what you got was someone good at being invisible.

Her hand drifted leisurely over her breast, her palm abrading the already stiff nipple. A rattling sigh escaped her lips, and a deep twist of liquid-hot wanting shot through her body.

She leaned her forehead against the tiled wall, her neck suddenly too weak to support her head, and took a deep breath, telling herself to calm down. She needed to pull it together before she saw him again.

She needed to remember who he was and who she was. Alike and yet different. Different in a way that she couldn't easily forget. She never had. She never would.

FIFTEEN

Niklas walked a hard line through the narrow hall of the B&B, calling himself every name he could think of for agreeing to a scheme that his every instinct screamed at him to avoid. He was breaking every promise he'd ever made to himself.

He unlocked the door to his room and slammed inside. Tossing his bag on the bed, he started packing, muttering to himself. He should just forget about Darby and the girl and go, leave. He would find Cyprian and kill him. He could do that better without them tagging along. *What was he thinking?*

Ten years ago, he'd begun this journey. No distractions, no companions or friends. Barely a man, he'd set out alone, his mother forever gone from him, lost to her demon. But the memory of her, of all she'd sacrificed for him, spurred him on.

He'd vowed revenge against those who infected him, on the one who forced his mother into making such a sacrifice.

And now look at him. He had a kid and a woman for companions. No, even worse than that. He had an *infected* kid and a white witch. A white witch whose very scent drove him mad with lust.

The irony wasn't lost on him that the first woman to get beneath his skin was a white witch. The very thing his mother was . . . the thing that she *had* been. Before she was taken from him.

He slung his bag over his shoulder and grabbed the gear he'd left scattered about the room. He'd need to stop and restock on ammo and supplies on the way out. He wondered if Darby even knew how to shoot. He'd probably have to give her some instruction on that. Which only irritated him more. The last thing he needed was to take time out for shooting lessons—and he definitely didn't need proximity to her. Thoughts of touching her already consumed far too much of his mind.

HIS MOUTH KISSED A *fiery path down her throat, teeth dragging and nipping at her skin. He buried both hands in her hair, pulling her head back for his ravaging mouth.*

A deep ache tugged inside her belly, throbbing and squeezing for relief.

He settled his weight between her legs, his hardness prodding against the inside of her thigh. She opened herself wider for him and slowly slid her hand between their bodies, enjoying the sensation of him against the back of her hand, the belly that was ridged with muscle and satiny skin.

She seized the hard length of him in her hand and ran her thumb over the tip of him. He shuddered over her. His cock filled her palm, pulsing and warm. Hot breath fanned her cheek as she guided him toward her, easing him inside her just a fraction . . .

Bang, bang, bang!

Darby bolted upright with a gasp.

She blinked and rubbed her eyes with a fist before swinging her gaze all around her bedroom, fighting the drugging influence of her dream . . . or vision.

Hell. Horror washed over her, dousing the heat brought on by her arousal. She didn't quite know.

For the first time in her life she couldn't distinguish between dream and vision. The realization left her stunned, shaken and furious with herself. For once in her life, her "gift" was proving unreliable. The one thing she could count on—whether she liked it or not—was the reliability of her visions, the recognition of them for what they were. And now she didn't even have that.

The banging at her door continued. She stumbled from bed, casting a glance over her shoulder to see Aimee still asleep, her face flushed, dotted with perspiration. The incessant knocking didn't rouse her in the least.

Darby peered through the blinds, verifying who was on the other side of the door. With a deep breath and silent command to forget her vision—dream, whatever—she pulled open the door.

Niklas stalked inside. "Didn't you hear me?"

"I was asleep," she mumbled, smoothing a hand over her wild hair self-consciously and hoping he didn't read more into the blush staining her cheeks.

"You're going to have to toughen up . . . especially considering where you're headed."

She straightened her spine. "I've hardly led a rosy existence. I'm tough."

He ignored her comment. "How's the girl?"

"Aimee," she ground out. She motioned to the bedroom. "Still asleep. Feverish like you said."

"Okay." He nodded. "Do you have your things ready?"

"Yes." She'd packed before she fell into bed.

"Good. Let's go. I have everything we need. She can sleep in the car. We need to move out before Cyprian's trail grows cold."

Ten minutes later, they were secured in the comfortable leather seats of Niklas's Hummer, the heat blasting on high. She sat in the back again,

Aimee's head cushioned on her lap. She stroked her light brown hair, trying to give the child, as she whimpered in her sleep, as much comfort as she could.

They pulled out from the back lot behind Sam's diner onto Main. As they approached the first stoplight, Darby surveyed Niklas through the rearview mirror. He looked left and right, considering which way to go.

"You know which way?"

He stopped looking and closed his eyes. The light turned green and still he sat there several moments before raising one finger and dropping it in the air to their right. "That way."

"Just like that? You know?"

"Yeah."

As they drove on, Darby turned and looked over her shoulder at the town she was leaving behind. A town like so many others where she'd worked and lived during the last few years. She felt no remorse.

Facing forward again, she looked down at the sleeping girl and vowed to make everything right for her. She brushed a hand over the girl's forehead. She would see Aimee made it to her grandmother safely. Looking up, she caught Niklas staring at her through the mirror.

He didn't look away immediately but seemed

to hold her gaze. She tried to read something in those indigo eyes, tried to see something there. She had thought they were alike, but now she wasn't so convinced. Now she wasn't sure she could ever know someone like him. Someone who quite clearly didn't want anyone to know him.

Sixteen

They drove late into the night before stopping at a motel. Niklas carried Aimee inside and laid her on the bed. Darby busied herself getting the girl tucked in. She seemed a little more at ease on the comfortable bed, tossed from side to side less.

"You should get some sleep," Niklas advised, removing his jacket. She tried not to watch the way his muscles rippled beneath his black sweater, but it was a point of fascination for her. She couldn't stop the surge of longing. She closed her eyes in a tight blink and looked away. She really was pathetic. This mission wasn't about her and her misplaced desires. It was about doing what was right for Aimee. Giving her the chance Darby never had.

"Yeah." She nodded, wrestling off her boots. "Sounds good." And she really was tired—drained even though all she had had to do was sit in the backseat, silent for the most part, her hands full of Aimee, stroking and petting and lending what comfort she could.

Her few attempts at conversation had been shut down. Or rather ignored. Niklas wasn't interested in talking. It hardly seemed he was interested in her. It was hard to imagine they had ever shared that kiss. Hard to imagine that he might have ever wanted her even for those brief moments.

So stop imagining it, a small voice commanded inside her.

Sighing, she doubted that would ever happen. Not as long as they were thrown together like this. Maybe not even when this was all over and they went their separate ways.

NIKLAS WATCHED AS SHE gathered her things and moved into the bathroom. He picked up the remote control from the table and forced his gaze away from the closed door and thin glow of light from beneath it. Punching the power button, he flipped channels until he found a news station. Something to do. Something to do to help block the screeching thoughts inside his head. Whirring thoughts that consisted of *her.* Darby, Darby, Darby.

He surfed for a local news channel. He always paid close attention to the news. The latest crime might be more than it appeared. It might be Cyprian. Although he doubted the alpha was doing too much damage at the moment. He was in flight mode now.

He shifted on the motel's uncomfortable chair. Usually he acquired better accommodations for himself, where he could at least get a good bed, but they were in the middle of nowhere, and this was the first motel they'd come across. Distant trucks roared past on the highway outside.

Splashing noises drifted from the small bathroom, mingling with the busy sounds from outside. The child whimpered on the bed. If he closed his eyes, he could almost pretend he was someone else, somewhere else. Just an ordinary man with a family. A kid napping on the bed, his wife washing up in the bathroom.

He squeezed his eyes in a tight blink and scrubbed his hands over his face—*hard*. He didn't want that. Didn't need those images imprinted on him. He'd only ever wanted one thing and it wasn't that. Not that crazy fantasy.

The sound of water stopped and she reemerged. She looked at him only fleetingly, her gaze avoiding his eyes, skimming him as she rubbed her hands dry on a hand towel. Her attention went to Aimee the precise moment the girl's small body arched off the bed, as though she was trying to escape from something inside her. And she was. Niklas knew that for a certainty. The memory of his Initiation might be foggy, but he remembered the pain, the misery. The death of himself.

"Shhh," Darby soothed, dropping down on the bed beside Aimee.

Almost in answer, Aimee whimpered and tossed her head side to side on the pillow. She cried out gibberish but one word rang loud and clear. *Monsters*.

Darby smoothed her hand over her brow and spoke as if the child could hear her. "No monsters are going to get you."

Niklas snorted, noticing she didn't deny the existence of those monsters.

She continued, "You have me and Niklas . . . and he's really strong. Almost as strong as they are."

Almost, Niklas thought with a wry twist of his lips. He fought back a bitter laugh. He was *almost* a monster.

"Trust us, baby. We're going to get you to your grandmother's. You'll be safe there."

At this promise, Niklas bit back a curse and quietly left the motel room. He strode through the cutting bite of wind, preferring the cold to staying inside the small motel room, listening to Darby make promises she had no right to make.

Still sheltered on the covered walk, he stopped in front of his Hummer. Snow already gathered on the hood. He cast a glance up at the sky, hoping the weather let up and didn't slow them down tomorrow. In the night beyond, he could make out the vast snow-covered mountains.

With any luck, they'd reach Edmonton tomorrow . . . and he knew he'd find Cyprian there. He felt it like he always did. Deep in his blood, in his bones . . . in the core of him where the beast prowled. He would always be linked to Cyprian. A link that he loathed, a link that he hoped to finally sever. And then, maybe, he would finally be free.

Cyprian was probably holed up somewhere, waiting out the month and assessing who to draw into his web as his newest pack member.

His hand knotted into a fist at his side. He had to reach him first. He was closing in. He could taste it. At last. After all these years. He could let nothing get in his way. Nothing and no one.

His gaze drifted back to the motel room as he considered the two females inside, and then his gaze strayed to his vehicle again. It would be a simple matter to leave them. He could make better time without them as they would only slow him down. He could finish Cyprian off and end Aimee's curse. He didn't need the girl with him to accomplish that feat.

But what if Cyprian slipped away? Eluded him one more time? Then the girl would be out there, on the loose, a little monster wreaking havoc— possibly even harming Darby. Unless Darby managed to stop her. And he doubted Darby possessed the strength or cold-blooded nature to finish her off.

"Thinking about leaving us?"

The sound of Darby's voice startled him, but he showed no sign of it as he turned to study her. She stood in the open door of the motel. Her hazel eyes wise and knowing as she surveyed him with an arched eyebrow several shades darker than her auburn hair.

He said nothing at first, merely held her stare, annoyed at how close she had hit the nail on the head.

Finally, he retorted, "And end this good time we're having?"

Color surged in her cheeks. "Go ahead and laugh, but this isn't a joke to me."

"Oh, it isn't a joke to me either," he bit out, advancing on her. He swiped a hand through the air. "Everything about this is wrong." He looked her up and down where she stood shivering on the covered walk. "But you don't want to hear that. You won't."

"You think I want to be in this situation? That I enjoy forcing myself on you when you so clearly don't want to help me?" She stormed away from him, her hair whipping behind her like a fiery banner. She was almost to the door to their room before she swung back around. "I wish none of this had happened!" She waved wildly to the room where Aimee slept. "That little girl in there is seven years old! I'm twenty-seven. The same age as my mother when I was seven." Her eyes shone in the dark like polished glass. "That could be me in there! It *was* me!"

"Is that what this is about?" he growled, stepping toward her. He reached for her arm, but she yanked free, shaking her head fiercely.

"No! Yes!" She made a sound, part groan, part sob, and buried her face in her hands. Lifting her face, she glared at him. "I don't know!"

"Don't confuse yourself here, Darby." He pointed to the room where Aimee slept. "You're not that girl in there. And you're not your mother either," he bit out.

"My mother did it for me."

He shook his head, confused. "Did what?"

She continued, "My mother killed herself, removed herself from my life so I'd be safe. Don't you understand? If something happened to her . . . if she gave in to a demon, I'd be the one caught in the crossfire. How long before the demon possessing her turned on me? Seconds? Minutes? She killed herself to protect me!"

Her words hit him like a fist. He'd never known how alike they were. "So you've appointed yourself Aimee's protector to play out some sort of weird reenactment?"

Darby looked at him bleakly, the tip of her nose turning pink from the cold. "Aimee has no one."

He took another sliding step closer. "And what about you? Who has you?"

Her jaw tightened. "I don't need anyone." She shook her head and looked away.

For some reason the words created a pang in his chest. He didn't know why. Since he'd lost his mother—since he'd lost himself—being alone was all he knew. It had never bothered him. Someone else suffering loneliness had especially never bothered him before. He didn't need anyone. Why should he care that she didn't either?

He lightly cupped her cheek, forcing her to look at him again. "Yes, you do."

"And what do you know about needing somebody?" she whispered. "I don't exactly see you surrounding yourself with people. When was the last time you had anyone in your life?"

He stared at her, unable to speak. He couldn't even breathe, he wanted her so badly right then. He dropped his hand from her face.

"That's what I thought," she finished. "You're no different from me. You don't need anyone either."

She started to move away then, but he couldn't

let her go. Not yet. He snatched hold of her, wrapping a hand around the soft skin at the back of her neck. Her eyes widened for the barest second.

"I wouldn't say that," he growled, his gaze roving over her face.

And then he kissed her, smothered her gasp with the searing press of his lips on hers. The cold melted away as fire and heat erupted between them.

She held still for only a moment before coming to life and throwing herself into the kiss, pressing her body against him. He forgot everything in the taste of her, in the sensation of her body melting into his.

His hands slid along her cheeks, tugged through her hair, pulling her head back so that he could kiss her arching throat.

She roamed her hands over the back of his shoulders and up his neck, her nails dragging through his short hair.

"God, Darby," he moaned.

His hands grasped the collar of her button-down flannel shirt. He tugged. A button popped. Then another.

He broke their kiss to stare down at the swells of her breasts nestled in a black bra.

Gooseflesh broke out over her exposed skin from the frigid air, but it didn't matter, he couldn't stop. He cupped one mound, kneading and lifting it within the lacy black cup. He nipped at the top of the plump curve. He drew the pointed tip of one breast into his mouth, laving it with his tongue until the lacy fabric was wet and clinging to the turgid peak. She moaned, her fingers digging into his shoulders.

A car horn blared three times. They jumped apart. Niklas spun around. A car with a pair of giggling women rolled past. One rolled down the window to shout, "Get a room!"

He turned back around just in time to see Darby disappearing inside the room.

With a disgusted sigh, he dragged both hands through his hair and stared out at the lightly falling snow. He waited several moments for his lust to cool. When it became obvious that was never going to happen, he followed her back inside.

A faint glow of blue suffused the room from the television she'd turned on. Darby was in bed, curled up next to Aimee as if nothing had happened between them.

She ran her fingers through the girl's hair in a languid motion.

He eased down onto his chair. A movie played that he'd never seen before. Not that he spent a lot of time watching TV.

"This is my favorite part." Darby was whispering as if Aimee were awake and could hear her.

His gaze moved to the television and he watched as a girl in period costume was torn away from a man she called papa.

"You see," Darby explained, "he doesn't remember that she's his daughter because he was hurt in an accident. He can't remember anything anymore, not even himself. But keep watching . . ."

Just then the actor on the screen presumably remembered his identity and the identity of his daughter and took off after her through the pouring rain, sweeping her up into his arms. Grand music played in the background.

"And there." Darby's satisfied voice floated over the room. "He remembered. And they live happily ever after."

Darby glanced down, the smile slipping from her face as she eyed Aimee, still sleeping restlessly, her thin chest rising and falling rapidly beneath the bedcovers.

Niklas looked away, feigning interest in the movie and not this woman he was coming to understand. And like. It wasn't just lust—he liked her.

Her company was torture. On so many levels. He looked out the drab motel curtains that smelled faintly of mildew and told himself he was checking the conditions of the road and not struggling with every fiber of his being to ignore the woman a few feet away.

AIMEE SETTLED DOWN AFTER a while, her breathing easier, less raspy. Darby pressed a hand to her brow and gave a satisfied nod. She even felt less feverish.

With a relieved sigh, Darby carefully rose from the bed and grabbed her things. Deliberately not looking to the man who sat like a marble statue in the chair by the window . . . the man who had kissed her outside the motel room and left her confused. And hungry for more.

She slipped into the bathroom again.

Stripping off her clothes, she hesitated in the small space, shivering in her bra and panties, examining herself, trying to see herself as Niklas might. She winced, heat crawling up her face.

She couldn't help herself. She stared at the door. The flimsy particleboard. It was all that separated her and Niklas. Her belly tightened and her breasts ached, remembering his touch there. She shook her head and snatched her toothbrush from her small cosmetic bag.

After brushing her teeth—more vigorously than usual—and changing into a pair of pajama bottoms and top, she reemerged. He'd turned out the lights. It startled her for a moment, walking out into a darkened room, and she paused, her eyes adjusting.

The only light flowed through the tiny part in the curtains that let in an orange glow of the motel's perimeter lights. She made out his dark shape still in a chair by the window. She felt his eyes on her.

"You're not coming to bed?" She winced at the intimate sound of the question. For some reason the idea of him sitting in that chair in the dark as she slept made her uneasy. She'd have preferred he got into his bed and slept, too.

"I'll get some sleep in a while."

She nodded as if she understood or approved this. It was just a thoughtless movement because she didn't really know what to say to him. Or what to think. Or how to act. He was doing this great thing for them—he could have ignored her pleas and finished Aimee off. And she couldn't have really blamed him. His logic was correct. Which told her that some part of him had to be following his heart.

She slid into bed beside Aimee. Instantly, the girl's baking heat reached out to envelop her. She lightly grazed the child's arm. She was feverish again. Her skin burned and was slippery-wet with perspiration.

"You sure this fever will break?" She couldn't stop the worry from entering her voice.

"It will," he replied in that flat voice. "Initiation lasts a few days, but it will break. And she'll be a lycan when it's done."

Her jaw clenched at the reminder. He got it in every chance. Like she could ever forget. "She won't be a lycan until moonrise."

"Let's just say she won't be human anymore once the fever breaks."

She exhaled. She could handle that. What was Darby after all? A witch. What was he? Something *similar to* a lycan.

Neither were normal human beings. And they still deserved a chance, a hope for life. They were still struggling through each and every day. Like them, Aimeé deserved a chance, too. And Darby was going to make sure she got it. She wondered why Niklas didn't see it that way, too.

SEVENTEEN

Darby woke in the middle of the night. She wasn't certain what roused her, but her every nerve was stretched taut. She'd woken like this before . . . seemingly with no explanation to find there was a very real, very valid reason for her state of high alert. That reason was usually in the form of a late-night guest.

The demons never stayed too long when that happened. It was too cold, after all, for them to last beyond a few minutes. But they made the most of their time, tormenting her in an attempt to get her to submit. As a child they would send her sobbing in terror into her mother's room.

She squinted through the gloom, trying to see if a shadow worked its way toward her in the dark, slithering over the walls and floor. Goose bumps broke out over her flesh as her gaze scanned the room, darting around wildly, searching for any hint of something that shouldn't be there.

She clutched the three charms resting against

her chest and muttered a prayer low under her breath.

"What's wrong?"

She jerked at the low voice. Her gaze darted toward the bed across from her. Apparently, he did sleep. Or at least he relocated himself to the bed.

Niklas's eyes gleamed at her through the scant distance between their two beds. He slept shirtless. Her throat constricted at the sight of bare skin. Even in the gloom she could see the hard curve of his shoulder, the warm-looking male flesh, several shades lighter than the darker bedspread.

Her breathing grew tight and raspy, like she'd run a short distance at high speed, sprinting the last half mile on one of her runs. She couldn't help wondering what else he had on under those covers. Or didn't.

"What's wrong?" he repeated.

She inhaled slowly and evenly through her nose. "Nothing," she replied, her gaze once again darting around the room. Suddenly it seemed like a very good idea to look anywhere other than at him, so close, in that bed.

"Don't lie. Something's bothering you," he insisted.

Drawn against her will, her gaze slid back to him, taken aback at his insight into her—that he should know she was awake at all. How had he known that?

She drew a shuddery breath through her nostrils. Too bad it was the middle of the night . . . and her circumstances weren't more conducive. She could handle a run about now to quiet the worries in her head.

Something was bothering her all right. And it was him. Maybe that's why she was awake—why she felt so restless. It had nothing to do with a visiting demon. Instead it had everything to do with him. He was the different element. Him. *His nearness, his proximity, her hunger for him.*

"You sense something." Again, she felt that ripple of surprise that he should guess along those lines. But then she remembered that he would know a thing or two about witches. With his mother—what she was, what she had been—of course, he would understand her behavior.

"Nothing's wrong. Not really. I just woke abruptly, but I do that some times. Habit, I guess."

"Do they come to you at night?" he asked, clearly disbelieving her protests.

She said nothing for a long moment, considered pretending that she didn't even know what he was talking about, but then why bother? He knew. He understood.

She shrugged one shoulder. "Usually," she whispered, thinking of the slithering shadows that had pursued her over the years. She remembered each of them the moment they revealed themselves to her in their hideous forms. Shadows no more but their true shapes.

"C'mon. Talk to me, Darby."

And she wanted to. *God,* but she wanted to. She wanted to unburden herself, unload and share something, anything with another person on this earth. And not just anyone. Niklas.

"At night," she whispered, her fingers brushing her lips, marveling at how they still tingled from that kiss, how they tingled just because she was around Niklas, talking to him, confiding in him. "That's when I'm most vulnerable. When they usually come for me."

"And this is how you survive it?" He motioned with his hand, gesturing to the room, but she knew he meant the frozen, arctic world outside. "You live where they can't get to you?"

"My mom shot herself when it became too much. The demons appeared to her everywhere, every day. They were tormenting her, driving her mad. At the end, it was all the time. Day and night." She closed her eyes, almost hearing her mother's sobs and pleas through the walls again, begging for them to leave her alone. "She couldn't keep a job because her employers thought she was some freak, jumping at every shadow, talking to empty space. Breaking down in tears. But why am I telling you this? Your mom was one of us."

"Yes." He nodded. "She was."

Was. Darby stared at the hard line of his profile. "Then you understand?"

"It was never that bad for her. She was always happy to be alive. Happy to have me, happy for every day. I never saw her surrender to despair. They could have been bothering her. She just never showed it."

Darby grimaced. "You were lucky then. Maybe your mother was stronger. Or maybe they just really wanted my mother. She was a unique witch with multiple powers." She shook her head. "I don't know. Maybe Mom was just weak. My aunts are strong. They can ignore demons for the most part."

He slid her a measuring glance. "You're strong, too," he pronounced. "So why are you way out here all alone? Why aren't you with your aunts?"

She shifted uncomfortably. "My situation is different. I had to leave."

It felt intimate, almost cozy, both of them whispering to each other in the near dark. In their separate beds, but inches apart. If they stretched out their arms, they could touch hands, graze fingertips. She felt deceptively safe in this moment, as if they were more than two people thrust together out of necessity. As if maybe they wanted to be together.

And maybe that's why she confessed to him that very thing that had haunted her for so many years. "Once a demon took possession of me while I slept . . . and I tried to hurt someone. A—a friend—" Her voice broke as she recalled that moment she awoke years ago, holding a pillow over Sorcha's face. In that moment she'd known she had to go. Had to flee all her family and friends and live a life of isolation where she would never harm someone she cared about again. Since then, she'd never lived anywhere where water didn't freeze.

He cursed low. "Has it happened since then?"

She shook her head. "No. But I don't exactly surround myself with people. I can't risk it again."

"Maybe it was a one-time thing." There was no mistaking the ring of hope in his voice, and it warmed her heart that he would even care.

"Maybe. Or just living where it's so cold a demon won't visit for very long has kept them away." She sighed. Hope was a hard thing for her to manage. She hadn't felt hope in years. "Good thing I don't mind cold weather too much. I'd rather ski than surf any day."

His lips tipped in a teasing grin. "Well, then, nothing to cry about. It's no hardship."

She smiled. "Not at all. I live in a winter wonderland year round." Her smile slipped then. *Except for the loneliness.* Except for keeping everyone at arm's length.

"What are you going to do once you kill Cyprian?" she asked before she could consider how it sounded . . . how she sounded. As if maybe his future mattered to her because she wanted to be a part of it. She winced, hoping she didn't come off that needy or desperate. She hoped that he didn't think she was getting any ideas about them. They were both alone in the world, after all. Alike in many ways. It could be natural for the two of them . . .

His voice cut in, thankfully breaking her troubling thoughts. "I don't know. Haven't given much thought to anything beyond this." The bed rustled and she could make out in the gloom that he'd rolled onto his back. His chest rose and fell on a deep exhalation. "I guess I'll just continue to hunt other lycans."

She frowned. "Don't you ever want to try for a normal life?"

He snorted. "*Normal* isn't a word you could ever apply to me."

"But what about friends? Family? Don't you want any of that?"

Again, there was a long pause and she thought

he wasn't going to answer when he said, "I had all that once."

She guessed he meant when his mother had been around. She slid a hand between her cheek and the pillow. "And you don't want it again?"

"It's hard to imagine ever going back to that. Having that. Not when I'm this." She caught the motion of his hand in the dark.

"What?" she asked, the challenge ringing in her voice. "You're a lycan with a soul. Free will." She snorted. "You have control. Does that even make you a lycan? At least you're not limited to geography in order to maintain control over yourself—"

"You don't get it. You have demons taunting you to take a wrong turn. My demon is inside me."

And then she understood. That's why he'd never stop, never quit even after he'd killed Cyprian. He couldn't kill the beast inside him, but he could destroy others.

Suddenly the prospect of his continuing on after he killed Cyprian, traveling the world and hunting other lycans, living for nothing more than that, made her feel sad and hollow inside.

He watched her, his eyes narrowing, and she wondered if he could see her pity for him in her face.

Aimee made a small mewling noise in her sleep, sweet as a kitten. Darby rolled over and snuggled against the girl. The girl snuggled back, curving her little arm around Darby's waist. Her heart squeezed to have this, another soul close and receptive. She almost wished she could keep her and didn't have to hand her over to her grandmother. But that would be selfish. Darby firmed her jaw. She'd be fine.

Unlike Niklas, when this was all over, she would open herself to life again—to friends, to family. She couldn't keep living the way she had been. And she wouldn't think about him anymore. She wouldn't worry about him or feel sorry for him, wasting his life away, his heart cold and closed to love.

EIGHTEEN

It was dark the following day when they reached Edmonton, so they went straight to the hotel. It was late and no one thought anything of Darby carrying a sleeping child through the lobby and to the elevator.

Aimee had woken earlier that afternoon. It had been difficult to calm her. There had been no avoiding telling her some bare facts. She was smart and had lots of questions. It had to come out. At least an abbreviated version of what was going on. It was difficult for her to accept, but she'd seen those monsters, remembered the agony of her attack. She'd cried until no tears were left, her small body shuddering against Darby. Darby held her, rubbing her back, stroking her hair, assuring her that she wasn't alone.

I'm here. I'm here and not going to leave you. You're going to be okay.

Niklas and I are going to make everything right and get you to your grandmother. I promise, baby, we're not going to let anything else happen to you.

You're going to be all right.

As she'd uttered the words, she felt Niklas's stare on her through the rearview mirror. She felt those eyes, cold and penetrating, but she didn't meet his gaze—didn't dare look at him, guessing at the recriminations she would see there. She'd made a promise on his behalf. He didn't need to say anything for her to know that he didn't approve or appreciate the fact.

The suite Niklas procured for them was far more elegant than anywhere she'd ever stayed. On her wages it wasn't even a consideration.

"Why don't I order room service?" he asked after Darby tucked Aimee into bed in the second room. She closed the door quietly behind her and joined him in the lounging area, marveling how sitting in a car for hours could make her feel so weary.

She nodded. "Sounds good."

He scanned the menu. "Burgers okay?"

She nodded, flipping on the television, eager to do something—anything to occupy her hands. Anywhere to stare but at him. Hours in the car and he'd barely spoken two words to her.

She'd flipped through countless channels when he finally asked, "Are you going to settle on anything? You've passed every channel at least three times."

She lowered the remote to the sofa and shot him a glance. It was all he needed to begin.

"Don't speak for me again."

She knew instantly what he was referring to— knew why his jaw was set with tension. She'd pissed him off with that promise to Aimee.

"Would you rather I had not reassured her? Would you prefer I'd let her panic in the backseat of the car? I'm sure it would be an easy thing to travel with a hysterical child on our hands."

"Make all the promises you want, just leave me out of it."

She clenched her hands at her sides. "You can't just pretend . . . you can't just—just . . ." She waved her hands, fighting for words to express her frustration with him.

He arched a dark eyebrow.

She blew out a heavy breath. "You can't just disengage from us. You can't act like we're not here."

He looked her up and down, his gaze blistering. "Oh, I'm very aware that you are around. And the child—"

"Aimee!" She shoved to her feet and stamped her foot down. "You can't keep pretending that—"

He rose and moved on her in a blur of movement, his arm seizing hold of her arm and reminding her immediately of who she was dealing with. "Stop telling me what I can't do. You're here because I agreed to bring you along. I haven't had to answer to anyone since I was sixteen. I'm not about to start now."

"Fine," she bit out, twisting her arm free of his searing fingers but holding her ground—not backing down from his looming nearness. "Keep being an asshole," she blurted. The moment the words were out, she gasped at her boldness.

His lips quirked, which only made her angrier.

She pulled back her shoulders. "I don't like you very much."

He shrugged. "Why should you?"

"Don't mock me," she snapped.

"Who's mocking? We're not friends here. We're united in purpose. We have one mission here and once that's finished, we'll go our separate ways."

She shook her head. Her anger was still there, but buried beneath it was hurt, too. "Can't wait," she replied, giving each word a smack of decided relish.

He pressed his lips into a thin line. She felt a surge of satisfaction that he didn't look quite so ready to smile anymore.

An uneasy silence fell between them. She glanced around the room, sliding her palms along the thighs of her jeans. Finally, when she couldn't handle the tension anymore, she said, "I'm going to see if I can find an ice machine and soda. You want anything?"

She held her breath, forcing herself not to flinch beneath his regard, all the while fighting the memory of them together. Now, alone, Aimee no longer a comforting shield, she couldn't fight it. That kiss was there, a boulder in the room she couldn't ignore. And not just the kiss, but also that dream of them together. Yes, a dream. She had decided it had to be a dream. No way could it have been a vision. No way would his icy reserve thaw so that he took her to bed.

He stared at her coolly before shaking his head. "Thanks. I'm fine."

With a single nod, she grabbed one of the extra key cards and left the room.

She instantly breathed easier free of his proximity. Her steps fell silently down the carpeted corridor. As she passed one room, a man and woman's laughter floated on the air. For some reason, the sound made her feel only worse.

She didn't want to fight with Niklas. She wanted him the way he was before he knew what she was—before Cyprian and Aimee. When she was just a waitress . . . when he would watch her, talk to her, even smile a little—without mockery.

And, yes. Kiss her. He liked her then. She was sure of it. Now he couldn't wait to get rid of her.

She came to the end of the hall with no sight of an ice or soda machine. She blew out a breath. For all she knew, this floor didn't even have one. Not that it really mattered. She mostly needed an excuse to get away and clear her head.

She started to turn, hardly paying any attention to the fancy double doors of an executive suite to her left. Until one door opened and a man stepped out into the hall. Impossibly tall, broad of shoulder and lean-hipped, he commanded attention.

She stopped cold when her gaze met his. When she locked eyes with ice-cold pewter. Her chest tightened.

Another lycan.

She quickly told herself to act normal. He wouldn't expect her to recognize him for what he was. And he'd have no reason to harm her now, days after the full moon. Not when he was no longer in full shift and driven by hunger.

Still, her gaze must have lingered too long. She gave something away.

He arched a dark eyebrow and asked in a deep voice that struck her at once as refined and cultured, "Can I help you?" A faint accent clung to his words that she couldn't place.

She shook her head perhaps too fiercely. "No.

I just got turned around, I guess . . . looking for a soda machine."

He stared at her in an intense way that made her want to run. It brought to mind all the terror she and Aimee had endured, and she started to tremble.

With a curt nod for the dark-haired lycan, she turned and strode quickly down the long length of hall to their room. She pulled her key card from her pocket and fumbled to slide it inside the slot. She didn't look over her shoulder, didn't dare. But she felt him there. A great ominous force at her back, watching her flee. Her only thought was to reach Niklas and alert him to the lycan mere feet away.

She finally got the door open and shut. She fell back against the door, still shaking from coming face-to-face with a lycan. Here, several rooms down from them. As the reality of that washed over her, bile surged in her throat.

"Darby? What is it?" Niklas unfolded his lean frame from the sofa.

She pushed off the door and motioned behind her. "A lycan. Out there."

"What? Cyprian—"

"No." She shook her head, swallowing against the tightness in her throat. "Some other guy."

Niklas strode to a chair where he had tossed

some of his gear. "This is no coincidence, I'm sure. If this bastard is here, I'll bet Cyprian isn't far." He slammed a fresh clip into a gun as he pronounced this.

"What are you doing?"

"Going out there to introduce myself," he said, as if that were the most obvious thing in the world.

He tucked the gun into his waistband, letting his sweater fall over the weapon.

She blocked him as he moved toward the door. "You're just going to walk right out there? And what? Start shooting?"

"Let me pass," he commanded, his voice hard.

"You need to think this through. You have more to consider than yourself here."

For a moment, something flickered in his eyes and she thought her words had reached him. "Step aside, Darby."

Inexplicable fear clogged her heart, lodging itself there along with the disappointment his words caused. She shook her head no.

He must have read some of her feelings on her face, for he gentled his voice. "Darby, let me go. This is what I do. What needs to be done if you want to win Aimee back."

His words penetrated, broke through her resistance, her silly urge to keep him safe, close to her. And that was her true fear in his going out there.

She wasn't afraid for herself. She was afraid for him.

"Be careful. He's big."

"Bolt the door," he instructed, pulling the door open—and coming face-to-face with the dark-haired lycan waiting on the other side.

Darby clapped a hand over her mouth to drown out her scream.

NINETEEN

Niklas stared into the lycan's cold eyes and knew he'd never faced a lycan like this one before.

He instantly doubted this big bastard had any affiliation with Cyprian. He was too menacing, his eyes far too wise, cunning . . . ageless. Cyprian wouldn't keep such a male around in his pack. His presence would be too threatening, and Cyprian wouldn't jeopardize his position as an alpha.

"Can I help you?" he asked, his hand slowly drifting to the gun at his waist.

The lycan didn't remove his stare from Niklas's face. And yet Niklas knew that he knew. He knew Niklas was reaching for a gun, and he was ready.

His hand whipped upward, one finger held aloft in warning. "I wouldn't reach for that—not unless you want your next breath to be your last."

Niklas stopped the descent of his hand. For now. "What do you want?"

He nodded his head to Darby hovering just

beyond. "I want to know why the female over there looks at me like she has seen a ghost."

Those words just confirmed Niklas's suspicions. The lycan spoke with a quality that marked him as old. Older than any lycan he'd ever come across before. Niklas glanced uneasily over the lycan's shoulder. Where there was one lycan there would be more. They weren't solitary creatures.

"Maybe you look familiar." He shrugged and tightened his hold on the edge of the door, preparing to slam it shut, put a barrier between the lycan and the girls for however long he could.

"No. She looked at me like she . . . knows me."

And Niklas understood his meaning perfectly. He meant she looked at me like she knows *what* I am.

Niklas contemplated several ways this could play out, all the while realizing he had Darby and Aimee to consider. As Darby said, it wasn't just him anymore. He had to make sure they were unharmed. Damn. He'd never had to worry before. About anything or anyone. And now he did. Now he had to worry and he'd probably end up getting them all killed anyway.

All this would be for nothing.

Shit. Not if I can help it.

With that burning determination feeding him, he pretended to turn away as if intending to address Darby. Then, in as fast a move as he had ever made, he launched himself at the lycan.

Darby cried out as they tumbled out into the corridor. He seized his weapon and jammed it beneath the lycan's chin.

The lycan stilled beneath Niklas, his nostrils flaring as he sniffed. "Silver bullets, I take it? Now how would you know that?" His pewter gaze scoured Niklas's face. He inhaled, drawing in Niklas's scent. "You're not a hunter . . . but you're something. What? Not a dovenatu."

"Niklas?" Darby called from behind him.

"Close the door," he ground out, determined that she and Aimee be safe at least. "Bolt it."

"I'm not here to harm you," the lycan declared. "If I wished it, I could have already unarmed you."

"You could try."

"My point is that I wish you no ill."

"A *good* lycan not bent on killing?" he spat. "Whoever heard of that?" He deliberately ignored that that was essentially himself.

"My name is Darius." He nodded to the gun. "I would appreciate if you kept that silver bullet in its chamber. I don't mean you or—" His gaze flicked to Darby. She hadn't obeyed him. She still stood in the open door watching them. "Yours any harm," he finished.

"Niklas," she said in a low voice. "I don't think he's going to hurt us."

"She's right," Darius agreed.

"Darby, go inside." He cast her an annoyed glance. And that was the moment Darius chose to relieve him of his weapon. He surged beneath him and flung Niklas off, taking the gun from his hand in one smooth move.

Niklas hopped on his feet, ready to charge, inwardly cursing that he let Darby distract him.

Instead he stopped, froze when he saw the lycan stepping in the threshold and handing the gun to Darby.

"Here. I feel much more at ease with this in your hands. You seem the understanding sort." The bastard motioned inside the hotel room. "May I come in?" Without waiting for an invitation, he strode past a gawking Darby.

She looked at Niklas blankly before rushing back inside the room, no doubt remembering Aimee was asleep only a few feet away, defenseless.

Niklas followed. Darby stood anxiously, splotches of color marring her face, her fingers twitching nervously at her sides. The lamplight shone on her hair, setting it afire.

Darius moved with deceptive idleness, his animal power banked but there, present, humming near the surface. Niklas was not fool enough to think he should drop his guard simply because Darius had turned the gun over to Darby and claimed he meant them no harm. The fact remained that he was a lycan. And no lycan was good. They were all soulless, murder their only impulse.

His body tense, he eyed his gear several feet away as Darius strolled to the window that looked out over downtown. As if he weren't a monster and cared about the skyline view.

The lycan paused suddenly, angling his face like an animal sensing something on the air. He turned then in a sharp move and strode for the bedroom where Aimee slept.

Darby jumped in his path, pressing her hands to his chest as if he weren't a creature that could snap her like a twig.

"Darby!" Niklas flashed to her side, taking her place in an instant and shoving her behind him.

He and Darius stood nose to nose.

Something flickered in Darius's eyes. "You're not human."

"You're not welcome here," Niklas growled, feeling his own beast swimming beneath the surface of his skin. For a moment he considered unleashing it, setting it loose. "Leave now before this gets ugly."

Darius's gaze flicked toward the room where

Aimee slept. His eyes seemed to glow brighter in that moment. "What do you have in that room?"

"Nothing that concerns you."

Those pewter eyes turned back on him, sliding over him before moving again to Darby. "It's a lycan. Like me. I can sense her." He tilted his head and considered Niklas. "But you're something else. Not human. What are you, friend?"

"I'm not your friend," Niklas growled.

"If you're a lycan," Darby began as if there were any doubt, "then how come you . . . how is it that you aren't—"

"Aren't intent on killing you?" Darius finished with a shrug of one tightly muscled shoulder. "I've killed enough. Lived enough lifetimes where the stench of blood . . . death has filled my every waking moment. I suppose I've gained a sort of resistance. It doesn't affect me as it once did."

Bullshit. "You lie," Niklas spat. "A lycan cannot control what he is." *Except for me.* He was the exception.

The very notion that this . . . *Darius* had some control over his actions enraged him. It meant that his mother hadn't needed to sacrifice herself. It meant that if Niklas had been strong enough, she would still be here. The urge to commit violence against the lycan standing before him consumed him.

He felt the beast surge up inside him then. He fought it, struggled against it, denying that part of himself—but never had the struggle been this hard.

Darby placed her hand on his arm, the message behind the slight touch of her hand clear. She wanted him to still his impulse, to stay his hand. He looked down into her hazel eyes. *She believed the bastard*. Believed that he wasn't a murdering monster like Cyprian. Like every other lycan on this earth.

Suddenly, Darius's cell phone rang and he answered it as if he weren't among enemies at all—as if he were just paying them a social visit. "Yes . . . yes . . . all right. Gather the team and I'll be downstairs in five."

The team? "Your pack?" Niklas growled, shaking off Darby's hand and darting a glance to the large duffel on the chair where his weapons were stowed.

Darius smiled. "Not like you think. But we're a force of sorts. I'm the only lycan among them, however, so calm yourself. We're on the hunt for . . . something."

"What?" Darby asked.

Darius's gaze fell back on Darby, lingering there with an interest that made Niklas's muscles bunch and tense.

"A witch."

Darby gasped, the color bleeding from her face as she staggered back a step. None of which was missed by Darius. The lycan looked at her with more interest than ever, his gaze searing and intense. Suddenly that gaze fell, dropped to her neck—to the necklace she wore there.

Niklas bit back a curse and forced himself to not snatch the necklace from her neck and hide it from sight. That wouldn't exactly be the discretion he was going for. It was too late, anyway. The lycan had already seen it.

Darius reached out and lifted the three charms that dangled on the end of her chain.

"Salt. Holy water and milk." His eyes shot back to her face. "To help ward off demons, I presume. Does it help?" He looked at her so intently that Niklas suddenly knew that this lycan knew what she was—had figured it out just as he had.

"For the most part," came her breathless reply. "That, and living in arctic temperatures seems to do the trick."

"So I've heard," he murmured.

"I take it you're hunting a demon witch. Why?"

"Not just any demon witch. One."

Understanding lit her eyes. "You're after *her*."

"After who?" Niklas demanded, his every muscle tensing at the mention of a demon witch. His mother was out there somewhere, running around performing a demon's errands all because of him. Beyond help. Beyond saving. At the mercy of a demon. Naturally he wondered if they were talking about his mother. Could this Darius be after her?

"Who are you talking about?" he repeated.

Darius ignored his question. A slow smile curved the lycan's mouth as he surveyed Darby. "Smart little witch, aren't you?" He nodded once, seemingly satisfied. "What's your particular gift? Something useful, I imagine?"

Instead of answering him, she said, "You can't kill her, you know. Not without potentially screwing us all. If you're truly good, how can you want that?"

The corner of his mouth tipped. "I never said I was *good*."

She scowled. "It's not true, you know. Killing a demon witch doesn't reverse her curse."

Niklas blinked in surprise at this statement, even if Darby was alleging it to be untrue.

She continued, "If you kill a demon witch, you unleash her demon on the world. Plain and simple. The demon will roam freely in corporeal form!" she reminded Darius sharply.

"Yes." He cocked his head consideringly. "I have heard this." He nodded his dark head in a mild way, clearly unaffected by the possibility. "I don't believe it though."

"What don't you believe? That killing her will free her demon? It's true. And there's no proof that once you kill the witch, her curse lifts."

Niklas whipped his gaze to Darius. "Is that true? If you kill the demon witch who started this curse, you end the lycan curse?"

"No!" Darby snapped. "Don't listen to him. There's no evidence this is true. It's a myth."

"There are many myths," Darius countered, that slow smile there again. "Myths of lycans, witches, demons . . ."

Angry color flooded Darby's face at this well-made point. "Well, *your* theory is truly myth."

"I believe the answer lies in finding Tresa."

"Leave her be," she insisted, spacing out her words.

"I can't do that." He motioned a hand, encompassing himself it seemed, or maybe the world at large. "She's responsible for all this and for whomever you're hiding in that room that you're trying to shield from me."

Darby stiffened and scooted to position herself closer to the door, the fear once again all over her face that he would go after Aimee.

"Well," Darius pronounced in that eerily polite way. "As delightful as this has been, I must be on my way. Sorry to barge in on you both." He looked at Darby. "And I'm sorry if I frightened you."

Niklas returned to himself then, asking himself if he was really going to let this lycan leave. Lycans deserved death. This was a rabid animal that needed killing.

His hand moved to his weapon. Darby's hand met his there, her chilled fingers covering his, stopping him. She shook her head swiftly at him.

Her presumption nearly pushed him over the edge . . . until he reminded himself he never fell off any edges. He never lost control. Could never take such a risk. Never would.

The lycan was almost out the door when Darby rushed over to him and boldly laid her hand on his arm. Something burned up inside Niklas at the sight. He had to force himself not to move, not to react.

"Please reconsider," she pleaded. "Leave Tresa alone. If you're truly the reformed lycan you claim to be, then leave her be. You can't risk humanity."

He smiled again and there was a touch of sadness there—if such a thing were possible for a lycan. "My existence is a risk to humanity."

"So that makes it okay to risk mankind even more?" Niklas couldn't stop his disgusted snort. If this lycan could decide not to kill and feed, then he could decide to leave one witch alone. Especially if doing so was the *right* thing to do.

At that moment, the temptation to put a silver bullet into the bastard hit him harder than ever. Darby's hand dropped from the lycan's arm and some of the killing hunger pumping through him abated.

The lycan lifted his gaze to Niklas, and it was so knowing, so smug—as if he knew that every fiber inside Niklas was urging him to violence. Clearly, Darius knew—he felt Niklas's rage, tasted it on the air. He knew. And not just because he was a lycan, but because he'd lured Darby in . . . because she'd touched Darius without fear—with an open heart.

With a final nod, Darius left.

Darby closed the door after him, hugging herself as if she were suddenly cold, bereft without the lycan's presence. Niklas's blood burned hotter, if that was possible.

"Don't ever do that again," he warned.

"Do what?" She blinked at him.

"Stop me from doing what I know I should do."

Her eyes narrowed with understanding, darkening, more brown than green at that moment. "Meaning kill Darius?" She spoke his name like they were friends or something.

"For starters." He nodded. "And don't ever

place yourself in danger like that. He was a lycan, a killer, but you seemed to have a hard time remembering that." He shook his head. "You *touched* him. I told you to hold silent. But what do you do? You insinuated yourself closer to a lycan."

"He wasn't a killer."

"I seem to recall him saying that he was. Did you not hear that little announcement?"

"Yes. I recall. I also recall he said he *was* a killer. *Was*."

He swiped a hand through the air. "Semantics. He's a lycan. Lycans kill. He did. He will again. It's not a switch he can shut off."

"You're a lycan," she flung at him, her words as sharp and well aimed as an arrow. "Are you a killer, too? Should I trust my life and Aimee's life to you?"

"I'm very much aware of what I am. A fact I battle every day. But I have control." He didn't shift. He resisted the pull of every moon. Unlike other lycans, he could shift whenever he wished. If he wished. And he didn't. He never would.

"And so, apparently does that guy. He didn't try to kill us." She waved an arm toward the door. "Can't you give him a break?"

"Why do you have to argue with everything I say?"

She expelled a heavy breath. "What do you

want from me?" She stepped forward to poke him in the chest with the sharp tip of her finger. "You want me to be a woman who meekly obeys your every whim? Well, sorry, but that's not me."

"I don't *want* you at all," he reminded her. "You're the one who insisted on tagging along with me. That being the case, I would think you'd do what I say or risk getting left behind on your ass."

She looked pissed now. Her features screwed tight. "You made a promise."

"As did you. I told you that it was my way or nothing. Do you recall that you agreed to follow my lead and do as I say?"

She blinked several times but said nothing. Her bottom lip jutted defiantly. She remembered. Her answer was in her silence.

At last, she nodded—two hard jerks of her head. He sighed and dragged a hand through his hair. "Look. It's late. We should just get some rest."

A knock sounded at the door. He motioned for her to stay where she was and looked through the peephole. A waiter stood there. Niklas opened the door, letting the waiter carry in the tray of food. He'd forgotten he even ordered anything. Signing off on the bill, he turned to find Darby gone.

He moved to the bedroom she shared with the girl. "Darby?" he asked quietly.

Her shadow hovered near the bed where Aimee slept. "I'm not hungry," she whispered quietly, dropping a hand on the nightstand and tugging off one of her shoes.

"You need to eat," he insisted, hating the guilt he felt for coming down so hard on her.

"Is that a command?" she returned, her words a deliberate dig on his reminder that she needed to do as he said.

"No. It's not." Turning, he left the room, feeling hollow inside, lonelier than he'd ever felt. Strange, he'd never felt *alone* before. Now that he was with Darby, he felt . . .

He felt.

TWENTY

An hour later, Darby couldn't deny she was hungry. Not too eager to run into Niklas again after the childish way she'd acted, she pressed her ear to the door to listen for the television. No sounds carried from the other side.

She should have just eaten when she had the chance, when the food was hot, instead of being so stubborn. Because he was right. She'd agreed to do as he said, to follow his lead. That had been the understanding when they first began this together.

She pulled open the door and peered out. The room was empty. The city skyline suffused the room with a dim glow. She moved to the tray and lifted the lid. Her burger and fries were still there, untouched.

Sinking onto the couch, she took a generous bite from her cheeseburger. It was cold but still satisfying to her growling stomach. She bit into a fry, then dropped it. That was one thing she couldn't eat cold. She took another bite of the burger and practically moaned. That was better than the first taste.

"So you were hungry."

She jumped where she sat and struggled to swallow her bite. Covering her mouth with her fingers, she said accusingly, "You scared me."

"How could I sleep with you out here moaning over your dinner?"

"You didn't hear me." She took a sip from the glass of water on the tray. He smiled and she knew he was teasing. She smiled back and took another bite. "Did you eat?"

"Yeah."

She inhaled through her nose, finished chewing and took another sip before saying, "I'm sorry. You were right. I promised to follow your lead and then I—"

"I didn't come out here for an apology."

"No?" She plucked at the burger bun, tearing bits of bread between her fingers.

"I couldn't sleep."

"Why not?"

His eyes gleamed at her in the near dark, and she felt herself leaning closer, remembering their kiss, want to relive it again. Wanting to *live*. It had been too long. Too long feeling dead inside.

He didn't move but his eyes lowered to her mouth. Her food was suddenly forgotten, replaced with a new kind of hunger. She dropped her hand to his thigh, his muscles tightened beneath her hand, and she loved that. Loved that she did that to him.

She angled herself so that her lips were a hair's breadth from his. She didn't know where her courage came from—maybe the fact that she might never have a chance like this with him again. Who knew what the month would bring them? She only knew she wasn't going to back down now. This could be her only shot.

The blood pounded so hard in her ears, she could hardly hear her words. "You don't have to sleep." Her fingers slid up his hard-muscled thigh. "Neither of us does." She looked up at him from beneath her lashes. "Not yet."

He released a ragged breath, not moving an inch as she closed her hand over the hard length of him, her palm pressing down on the erection straining against his pants. Air escaped between her teeth in a loud hiss as she tested the shape of him with her fingertips.

Warm fingers circled her wrist. Her gaze flew to his face, thinking he would stop her now. She drank in the sight of his strained face.

He didn't remove her hand from him. His grip on her shifted, guided her hand to move. Up and down. Up and down. His gaze scorched her, blistering her very soul as he worked her over him.

He swelled beneath her touch, doubling in size. Desire pooled low in her belly. She squeezed her thighs tightly together, attempting to relieve the growing ache between her legs.

"See what you do to me?" he asked, dragging her palm over him, faster, harder, the stiff feel of him making her breath come harsh and swift. God, she wanted him. Hard and swift. She wanted him to fling her back on the couch and take her . . . to let that animal part of himself go.

She longed to feel him without the clothes between them. She wanted to feel the texture of him, test the pulsing heat of him in the palm of her hand. No barriers.

Unbuttoning the top of his pants, she drew the zipper all the way down and slipped her hand inside. She closed her fingers over the naked length of him. Silk on steel in her hand. She ran her thumb over the satin-smooth tip of him. His groan tore through her, filled her with a heady delight.

"Niklas," she whispered, scanning his face, the square jaw, the hard lines and shadowed hollows. The throat that worked in speechless wonder at what she was doing to him.

His eyes blazed down at her, the fire there unmistakable. An answering flare burned through her blood, her soul, filling the emptiness, the lonely ache that had been there for too long now.

Lowering her head, she tasted him with her tongue in a deep lick. He shuddered beneath her and she licked him again, swirling her tongue around the head of him. She did this several times, feeling him tense and tighten beneath her like a winding coil. At last, she took him fully in her mouth, slid her lips down the length of him. He released a low cry, his hips thrusting to meet her plunging mouth.

She reveled in his groans, in the sensation of his hands tangling in her hair. He was hers. Totally at her mercy.

"Stop," he cried out brokenly, his strong hands clamping down on her arms and pulling her to him. He lifted her onto his lap and swallowed her sound of protest with his mouth.

He drank long and deep from her lips, obliterating her senses. His hands gripped her head, angling her for the onslaught of his lips. Then his hands moved, covered every inch of her until she was panting and moaning and rubbing herself against him, desperate to end the agony of wanting him.

His mouth kissed a fiery path down her throat, teeth dragging and nipping at her skin. He buried both hands in her hair, pulling her head back again for his ravaging mouth.

A deep ache tugged in her belly, throbbing and squeezing for relief.

She jerked with sudden memory. She'd seen *this, lived this* before. This was her vision. She had predicted this happening.

"Darby," he rasped, the softness of his lips against hers a direct contrast to the rough, guttural sound of his voice. "I didn't want this . . . I tried."

She shook her head, not understanding, not able to make sense of his words. The taste of him made her head whirl, spicy warmth in her mouth. Her shaking hands pulled his sweater over his head and caressed his sculpted chest.

Words were beyond her. There was only him. And the delicious way he made her feel. She didn't want to wonder if what they were doing was right or wrong. She didn't want to think about tomorrow . . . or the month's end. She wanted only to savor.

Her palms skimmed his firm chest, curving over warm flesh, velvet skin stretched tight over muscle and sinew. Incredibly, it seemed he was hers now. His body, at any rate.

He took her bottom lip between his teeth, nipping gently and murmuring against her mouth, "I don't care what I said." His hoarse voice stoked the heat in her belly into a nest of writhing flames. Pulling back, his hands skated up her arms. "I want you."

Relief rippled through her at his words. Because it would kill her to stop now.

His shining eyes burned fire in the room's dim glow, searing a path directly to her heart. "Tell me you want this."

Darby closed the one-inch distance separating their lips and kissed him with everything she had, letting him know exactly what she wanted from him. "There," she said, coming up for air.

He growled and hauled her against him, showering fierce kisses over every inch of her face before his mouth fell on hers in a savage kiss.

He lifted her in one sweep and carried her into his bedroom and dropped her on the bed. Still standing, he shrugged free from the rest of his clothes and stood before her as she had never seen any man. She'd never been with a man who looked like this. He was magnificent. All hard lines, curving muscles and shadowed hollows that made her mouth tingle, eager to taste.

He came over her then, his body a thrilling weight, hard and large upon her. Her hands roamed his broad back, nails digging into supple skin as he lowered his head to suckle one breast through the thin cotton of her shirt. Pleasure-pain lanced through her. His teeth abraded her nipple into a hard point, and she arched against him, crying his name. One of her hands tangled in his hair, urging him closer.

He turned his attention to her other breast, laving her nipple with his hot tongue, inching her pajama bottoms down as he did so.

Cool air licked her calves, her thighs, her hips. With startling deftness, he pulled her shirt over her head, leaving her bare and exposed before him. She shook with both desire and trepidation, overcome with the newness of his feasting stare on her naked body.

"Darby." His hand hovered above her abdomen, long fingers splayed wide, shaking ever so slightly. His hair fell over his brow, hiding his eyes as he studied her.

She didn't need to see his eyes to feel their heat, intent and searing on her. Slowly, his hand lowered to cup her between the legs.

She sighed and pressed herself up into his palm. He began to knead there and her breath caught in her throat. His gaze shot to hers. A sexy smile hugged his well-shaped mouth.

She stopped breathing altogether when his head dipped and he pressed a series of openmouthed kisses over her belly, working his way down to where his hand worked over her mound.

His warm fingers teased at her entrance, stroking, spreading her own moisture over her in erotic circles that dragged animal like sounds from deep in her throat. His finger plunged inside her then and she lurched off the bed with a ragged sob.

"Easy," he crooned, his touch magic as he worked her to a fever pitch. His eyes glowed brightly as he stared at her, twisting and writhing beneath him.

"Now," she pleaded, her head coming off the bed. Legs opening wide, she urged him to her. Her fingers trailed the line of his spine, cupping his ass in her hands and urging him inside her.

"Niklas," she pleaded, her voice low and desperate, unrecognizable even to her own ears.

"Darby," he moaned, sliding into her in one smooth thrust, filling her with stunning force.

For a moment, he remained still, lodged deeply inside her, pulsing in rhythm to the squeezing burn at her center. Every nerve in her body stretched and screamed, humming in sweet, agonizing tension as he held himself still inside her.

His biceps quivered as he restrained himself, hands braced on either side of her head. Gradually, he moved his hips, pumping slowly, torturing her with deep, unhurried strokes.

Her gaze devoured him above her, his beautiful olive-hued muscles straining over her in a way that made it clear he held himself tightly leashed.

His hair fell over his forehead in a veil, the dim lighting gilding those lighter strands. Her trembling fingers brushed it away, watching as it fell back with a will of its own.

Her body arched like a bow beneath his thrusts. She flexed her inner muscles around him. His groan filled the air and his thrusts grew harder, slamming into her, stoking the fire he had started within her that first night she saw him outside the store.

Higher and hotter the flames rose until her skin, her very bones, felt as though they would burst, leaving nothing but ashes behind.

"Niklas!" she cried, digging her nails into the smooth muscles of his back.

His head dropped to the crook of her neck. "That's it," he muttered beneath her ear. "Come for me."

One of his hands slid the length of her bare thigh, lifting her leg to better meet his thrusts. He pumped harder, deeper, the friction unbearable now, an exquisite pleasure-pain that drove her mad, left her gasping, sobbing, pleading incoherently.

But he understood. He knew just what to do. Answering her need, he hooked his thumbs beneath her knees and pulled back her legs for deeper penetration.

At last, she burst, exploded, shattered until she was a quivering pile of flesh and bones beneath him. Replete, sated, she sank back on the bed, content to still feel him over her, thrusting a final time with a loud shout of release.

A lazy smile lifted her lips. Rolling off her, he kept an arm loosely about her waist. She waited, unsure what to expect now.

Staring at the dark ceiling above her, she stroked his hard biceps, taking pleasure in the sound of his ragged breath near her ear, gradually slowing. She had done that to him—robbed him of breath, control. Pleasure suffused her and she snuggled deeper into his arms, her heart clenching when he tightened his hold on her in a way that made her think he would never let go. After a while his breathing eased and his hold relaxed.

Smiling, she closed her eyes and drifted away, joining him in sleep.

TWENTY-ONE

So leaving her wasn't going to be as easy as he'd thought.

Niklas winced as he trailed his fingers lightly through the thick mass of red hair spilling across his chest, reveling in the sensation of her body against his. Not that he had planned for this to happen. It wasn't as though he'd deliberately set out to sleep with her. He'd tried to resist. Still, it had happened.

She'd long since fallen asleep. He'd pretended to do the same. Cowardly, he supposed. He wanted to avoid any awkward after-sex conversation.

Not that he had ever felt awkward before. He'd never worried about conversation because there'd never been any. It had only ever been sex before. Just that. Only that. This, with Darby . . . Well, it was something else. Something more.

It was as though some part of himself had known once wouldn't be enough with her. That if he let her in, if he caved and got too close to her, he would be faced with this moment and the uncomfortable knot in his gut at the prospect of saying good-bye to her.

Part of him wanted to be mad, wanted to get out of bed and leave the intoxicating warmth of her body pressed flush against his own, but then there was that other part, the overwhelming voice in his head that told him to stay, to enjoy. Take what she offered him.

And that was more than her body, he realized. This hadn't just been about sex. There was need. In both of them. For some reason, he *needed* her. And he hadn't needed anyone, hadn't felt bonded to another soul since his mother. For years, he'd been alone and that had been just fine. Until he met Darby.

She sighed against his skin, her breath moist and warm and spiking his hunger for her all over again. She nestled herself closer. His hand moved from her hair to the warm curve of her hip. For the first time he began to think about a future after Cyprian.

He began to think of a future like this.

DARBY WOKE WITH A panicked jerk, screams reverberating in her head. It took her a moment to realize the screams weren't her own. She shook her head, shoving tangled strands of hair from her face. Years of waking to the sound of her own screams and she couldn't be too sure.

But these weren't her screams. They were Aimee's.

She and Niklas both bounded from the bed. As Niklas dove for a weapon, Darby raced from his bedroom and across the small sitting area, grateful that she'd slipped her T-shirt on during the night.

"Darby, wait!" Niklas roared, but she couldn't wait, couldn't stop. Not for anything. She had to reach Aimee.

Guilt stabbed her for ever leaving Aimee, for putting her own selfish desires before the child. The girl probably woke up frightened and alone. At least that was the hopeful, desperate thought that rolled feverishly through Darby's head in the second it took her to reach Aimee's bed. Her empty bed.

"Aimee!" She looked wildly around the room before plunging back into the sitting area. That's when the cold hit her, penetrated her, slapping against her bare legs. Snow blew into the room like powdery smoke.

Niklas stood there, armed with a gun in each hand—staring straight ahead where the window stood open, his expression coldly blank, void of emotion. And in that moment she knew.

"Aimee," she whispered faintly, inching forward, her bare feet sliding over the flat carpet. She shook from head to toe—and not from cold. Not from the cold at all.

Niklas's arm shot out to stop her from going too close to the open window. She stilled, froze, but not because of him. Her own fear held her in check—fear of what she would see when she looked out that window. Of what she wouldn't see.

Without a word, he moved to the window and peered out. And down. *Four stories down.*

Niklas turned and faced her. The cold look in his eyes told her everything she needed to know. Everything she couldn't bear knowing. She closed her eyes and turned her face away, as if she could turn from the horrible truth.

Her stomach lurched and she pressed a hand to her roiling belly. "I think I'm going to be sick."

"Darby," he spoke her name steadily, lacking emotion, and she wondered if anything ever reached him, affected him. The violent urge to slap him seized her. Not wholly fair, but it was there nonetheless.

He slid one of his guns into his waistband and approached her, his hand reaching for her as if he would comfort her. That, she couldn't endure.

"Darby," he repeated her name softly, and she was flooded with the memory of their night together when that same soft voice filled her ear with intimate whispers . . . when she'd conveniently, selfishly forgotten all about Aimee.

She shook her head against this memory and took a step back, holding up a hand. "No, no, damnit! No!" Even now, shaken with grief for Aimee, he was still clouding her thinking.

"I'm sorry." His voice was infuriatingly calm. "He took her. I should have seen it coming—"

"Then why didn't you?" she lashed out, uncaring at that moment that she was being unfair.

"I should have," he admitted even as he flinched. "They're linked. Even more than I'm linked to him. She's freshly infected. He's her alpha. He sensed her . . . and low on pack members, it makes sense that he'd come for her. He's desperate to grow his pack again."

Desperate enough to claim a seven-year-old child.

"Great!" She tossed up her hands and then knotted them into fists, feeling like punching something, hitting and slamming her knuckles into something until the pain in her heart faded to numbness. "We have to go after her. Now. Right away!" The nausea returned in full force. "I can't stand the thought of Aimee with him for even one minute. She must be terrified—"

He nodded, but there was something in his eyes.

A certain vague distance that failed to convince her that he thought they could save Aimee.

"Get changed," he directed. "We'll go while the trail is fresh. I imagine a seven-year-old will only slow him down. He won't run far. Especially if she's resistant. She'll draw more attention than he wants."

They dressed hurriedly, neither speaking to the other. A painful lump resided in her throat, making speech impossible. Which was for the best. If she spoke she might break down in sobs and she needed to be strong, needed to keep moving, keep going. For Aimee.

And there was nothing left to say to him anyway. Nothing at all.

THEY TROLLED THE STREETS for hours, through the remaining night and all day into late afternoon. They stopped only to get some food, and this at Niklas's insistence. He knew if it were up to her, they would have kept going.

"You won't be any good to Aimee weak from hunger," he told her, studying her stoic profile beside him. "How do you expect to face a lycan less than full strength?"

She didn't answer him—simply placed her order through the drive-thru and stared ahead through the windshield.

Soon they were back on the road, and she only spoke if she had a question regarding their hunt for Aimee. Which only made him feel guiltier.

He should never have touched her, never let her in his bed, his head. He'd vowed to resist her, but it had been useless. He felt her in his blood. His lips twisted. Like a disease.

He knew she thought she could have done something to save Aimee had she simply been there, but she was wrong. Even if she'd returned to her bed to sleep, she couldn't have stopped Cyprian from claiming Aimee. She was blaming herself needlessly, and he wasn't going to let her do it a moment longer.

When they returned to their hotel room, he shut the door solidly behind them and crossed his arms over his chest, leveling a stare at her. "Don't blame yourself," he announced.

"No?" She arched a brow, her voice full of bitterness. "Who am I supposed to blame?"

"Well, aside from the lycan who took her? No one. Bad shit happens, Darby. You should know that."

She turned her face away from him.

He pressed on. "If you had been asleep in that bed when he came for Aimee, if you had tried to stop him, he would have killed you. A lot of good you'd do her then. Maybe you should be grateful you were with me."

Her lips pressed into a mutinous line, but she said nothing, clearly processing this and, he suspected, recognizing the truth.

With a defeated sigh, she sank down on the sofa. "What now?"

"The closer the full moon, the better I can sense him."

Her head snapped up and she looked at him incredulously. "You mean we're supposed to sit around twiddling our thumbs while he has Aimee and is doing God knows what to her?"

"We'll still look. Every day."

"Every day?" Her voice lifted a notch. "You don't have much faith we'll find her soon?"

"I didn't say that."

Her gaze drilled into him, demanding the truth.

Niklas sighed. "He's gone deep. Maybe underground somewhere . . . but he hasn't left the area. That much, I know. He's still close. Close enough to find. And easier, the closer we get to moonrise."

Darby unwrapped her scarf from around her neck and shrugged out of her coat with stiff, staccato movements. "I can't accept this."

"I know it's not ideal, but he's not going to hurt her—"

"How do you know? Just because he won't kill

her doesn't mean he won't *hurt* her. He could hurt her countless ways while still keeping her alive."

"What do you suggest we do besides scouring the city? That's all we can do right now," he asked, his clenched jaw aching. "I'll find Cyprian."

"Before the full moon?" she demanded. "Because after that it's too late for Aimee."

He looked at her with an arch to his brow that implied, *Yeah, I know that. I told you that. I warned you.*

And he did. Of course. That's why he'd tried to kill Aimee that first night. Because he knew he could be facing a predicament like this—with Aimee lost and on the loose out there.

"Say something," she hissed. "I'm sure you want to rub it in that you knew this was going to happen. That we should have put her out of her misery that first night, right?"

He shook his head. "I'm not saying that at all." *He'd only been thinking it.* "I agreed to this. And we'll continue looking for her tomorrow."

Anger flushed her face. Without a word, she stalked past him and into the bedroom she had shared with Aimee, slamming the door behind her.

He glared at that closed door. Anger spiked inside him that *she* was so obviously angry with him. He understood that she was upset, but why take it out on him? He'd done nothing except make a promise he shouldn't have made in the first place.

He muttered low in his throat and knocked a lamp to the floor with a crash.

He shouldn't have promised that he could find Cyprian before the full moon. He shouldn't have gotten himself tangled with a woman and a kid. What was he thinking? He'd never had the time or need for such things in his life before. And he refused to now.

TWENTY-TWO

She wasn't sticking around.

Adrenaline pumped through her as this decision surged through her veins to her head in a scary, burning rush. Her hands trembled as she shoved her hairbrush into her bag.

She spun around, searching for the rest of the few things she'd brought with her. Clothes mostly, but she knew she would need everything she had where she was going. She checked her wallet, counting her cash. She didn't keep a credit card. As much as she moved around, it was easier to just live on cash.

She knew what she had to do—what needed to be done . . . even though she'd always sworn to never consider doing such a terrible thing. Even her own mother killed herself to avoid such a fate. She'd only surrendered when the demons had become too much, tormenting her and driving her mad. As much as she resented her mother's actions, a small part of Darby had always respected that her mother had never caved to the pressure that demons placed upon her.

Her throat grew tight, air hard to draw into her lungs. Unbelievable as it seemed, the moment had come when the prospect seemed not only palatable but necessary. The sacrifice would be worth it. Aimee deserved a chance at life. She'd endured so much already.

The door to her bedroom flung open.

She spun around with a gasp, plunging her hands behind her, stopping them from fumbling through her luggage and alerting Niklas to the fact that she was leaving. "Ever heard of knocking?"

He stalked into the room and stopped before her, his face fierce, the silvery light back in his indigo eyes. "We need to get a few things straight."

She swallowed, not liking the hardness in his voice or the way his jaw clenched. He was pissed.

"Yeah?" She swallowed.

"What you're doing is wrong."

Panic fluttered in her belly. He knew she was leaving?

She lifted her chin, determined nothing he said—or *did*—would stop her from going, from doing what needed to be done. "W-what are you talking about?"

He jabbed a finger in the air, inches from her

nose, before continuing, "Blaming me, blaming you—it's just pointless, Darby."

He didn't know. She sucked in a deep breath and glanced away, trying to keep the guilt from her eyes—because her decision had been reached. She'd leave tonight. While he slept. Before he woke.

"There's no point arguing about this. Whether I blame myself, you . . ." She shook her head. "It changes nothing."

But he didn't look like he was finished. Which was really too bad. They stood toe to toe, their angry breaths the only sound in the room.

If this would be the last time she saw him, she regretted that it was like this. She turned, unable to bear the sight of him any longer. It just made it too much . . . too hard.

His hard hand clamped down on her arm and hauled her back around. Her body slammed flush against him and his mouth came down over hers, devouring, moving and firing instant heat and sensation to every nerve in her body.

It took her only a second to respond.

As it sunk in that this would be her last night with Niklas—last sight, last touch, last taste—she threw her arms around his neck. Perhaps this would be her last chance with any lover of her own choosing at all.

She plastered herself against him and stood on her tiptoes, aligning herself against him, her every curve fitting so naturally to him.

He growled low in his throat and lifted her effortlessly off her feet. They traveled only a few steps before she was falling, descending. He came down over her on the bed, his solid body thrilling in its power and weight upon her.

He kissed her mouth, her neck, his teeth grazing the sensitive flesh of her throat until she was moaning and arching against him.

Her hands wedged between them so that her fingers could access his clothes and tear at the fabric of his shirt with a desperate need. This, now, was everything. In this moment, she could forget the pain, forget what was and what was yet to come.

Buttons popped and flew through the air. A voice in her head told her to slow down, to enjoy and memorize this moment, the last she would have. But it was that same voice which made her rush greedily ahead and seize this, him—a memory to keep her warm for generations of lonely, bitter cold.

His hands moved with more finesse but were no less quick. Everywhere he touched, she burned, felt alive, connected to another soul.

She cupped his face in her hands, stilling for a

moment. Her palms flexed over his cheeks, reveling in the rough scrape of his bristly jaw. She gazed up into his eyes. The light there was nearly blinding, and she marveled that she'd done that to him. She'd brought out that desire in him. The intensity of his gaze stripped her of everything, made her feel bare and exposed—as if he could see to the core of her. All her secrets . . . including the terrible thing she was about to do. *She had to do.*

"It's going to be all right, Darby." His voice stroked her like the brush of a feather. His fingers brushed her cheek with such tenderness that a sob rose up in her throat. "We're going to find Aimee."

Staring into his beautiful face, she wanted to believe that. Wanted it to be true. And maybe . . . maybe it was.

But it was a chance she couldn't take.

She wasn't going to gamble with Aimee's life. Not when every moment that passed, a piece of her might be dying at Cyprian's hands.

She knew what she had to do. She saw it so clearly—even as she saw herself in Aimee. Alone. Motherless because her mother couldn't protect her, help her . . . Just like Darby's own mother, Aimee's mother hadn't even been able to protect her.

Luckily, Darby had her aunts to take her in.

Darby shuddered to think what would have happened to her without her aunts. She would never have made it.

Aimee had no one. No one but Darby.

And Darby knew. She had to be there for Aimee. Had to do this thing for the girl. A girl who had a shot at a normal, happy life. The life Darby could never have.

Deep down, she had still been hoping, kidding herself that she did have a chance. Why else was she trying so hard to live, struggling with this cat-and-mouse existence that wasn't really living at all?

She came up on her elbows and kissed him then, putting everything she had into it. Everything she ever had to give.

His hand delved between her thighs, playing against her, locating the little nub buried in her folds and rubbing, pressing, squeezing until she bucked against his hand.

She whimpered, thrusting her hips to meet him. He eased a finger inside her, working it slowly in, stretching her until a low moan spilled loose. Ducking his head, he claimed her lips, taking the sound deep into his mouth. He drank greedily from her, his kiss deepening, slick tongue sliding against hers in a sinuous dance.

She moaned as his finger withdrew, her hips

moving forward, seeking. Her core burned, ached with need.

He tore his lips from hers with a broken gasp. Their heavy breaths mingled between them, warm as vapor. He dropped his forehead to hers, his glowing eyes probing, seeking, reading her hunger for him in her own unblinking stare.

Then she felt him pushing inside her. She hissed at the burning pleasure, the searing stretch of her inner muscles. Deeper, he penetrated her, and the pleasure grew, expanded.

With a groan, his fingers seized her hips, anchoring her for his repeated thrusts. She cried out at the swift, pounding pleasure.

One of his hands flew to the back of her head. His mouth was on hers again, feverish and hungry. He kissed her until the ache between her legs grew to a desperate throbbing, matching the pulsing rhythm of his body slamming into her own.

Her legs parted wider without will or volition. He kissed her until she could no longer feel her lips. Until breath eluded her, unnecessary as long as she had him. His mouth, his hands . . . his body merged with hers.

His hand fell on her breast, his fingers finding the peak, rolling and squeezing her nipple until it turned into an aching little point. She writhed beneath him, dark, desperate sounds escaping her lips. She tangled a hand in his hair, pulling roughly on the strands.

He rewarded her, sliding his hand between them and rubbing that spot. She broke free of his lips with a sharp cry. She lifted her calves and locked her ankles around his hips, rocking against him.

His eyes stared down at her, more silver than indigo in the dim light. She clenched her inner muscles around him in repeated clutches. Moaning, he dropped his head to the crook of her neck and began moving. Fast and fierce, thrusting in and out of her, pounding with unchecked savagery, the beast in him unleashed.

And still she wanted more. Wanted all. Head tossing back, a scream poured from her lips, drowned out as his mouth covered hers. She shattered inside.

Ripples of delight washed over. She trembled as he pumped into her, the smacking sound of his body against hers thrilling and primitive. With a shudder and deep groan of his own, he finished, pouring himself deep inside her.

Panting from exertion, she flexed her fingers where they clutched his head, holding him close as the pain, the grief slowly returned.

The remnants of desire gradually ebbed from her body, faint tremors playing out along her nerves. She trembled as he lifted his head, his gaze colliding with hers. Still lodged inside her, she felt him pulse, twitch. The sensation was surreal and not a little intoxicating. It was almost as though they were one being. Connected. A bond she had never felt before. From the intense gleam in his eyes, he did not appear eager to sever that connection.

For moments, they did not move, did not stir beyond their chests rising and falling with matching breaths. Staring into his eyes, her fingers curled in the impossibly silken strands of his hair, she wished that she never had to move, never had to break the magic of the moment. She closed her eyes in a pained blink. An impossible dream. She knew what fate awaited her—what must be done.

TWENTY-THREE

Long after Niklas's breathing eased into sleep, Darby lay awake, listening to the sound of him beside her, enjoying the sensation of his smooth, warm skin pressed against her, committing this to her memory alongside everything else, etching this night and her every encounter with him into her very soul. She had to make it enough. Enough to last forever.

She traced light patterns on his chest with her fingers. Now she understood. People weren't meant to be alone. They weren't built for solitude. *She wasn't*. That's why everywhere she looked she saw families, couples. That's why she felt a pang in her heart when she watched them.

A sigh rippled past her lips, and she snuggled deeper into his warm shoulder. She could have grown accustomed to this. Could have learned to love sleeping in a bed every night with this man. The injustice of it all made bitter tears prick her eyes. She wanted this. Wanted him. And for more than one night. She conveniently didn't consider that he may not have wanted a future with her. She was playing out a fantasy here.

She stared into the inky dark, her eyes wide open even as she registered that she was growing tired. Sleep wasn't to be hers tonight. She'd sleep enough later. Or not. Either way long years yawned ahead of her. Tonight she wanted to engrave every moment with him—like this—inside herself.

An hour later, when she could delay no longer, she slipped from the bed and dressed herself, keeping her gaze trained on Niklas, making certain he didn't wake.

His sculpted chest rose and fell as he snored gently, one hand thrown carelessly above his head. He didn't budge.

She moved with stealth, careful not to make a sound. Gathering her coat and bag, she paused at the bedroom door, feasting her gaze on him a final time, her mind whispering a silent good-bye.

Lifting her arms, she removed the necklace from her throat. She stroked the three charms for a moment, letting each of them glide between her fingers for the last time. They'd been more than her protection these many years. They'd been a comfort to her for so long now—something her mother had given her when she'd turned thirteen. Her neck felt naked without the chain there.

She delicately placed the necklace on the bed-side table. It hadn't been foolproof protection over the years, but she knew it had helped. Tearing her gaze away from the talisman, she hurried away on silent feet before Niklas woke and persuaded her to change her mind.

As shaky as she felt inside, she doubted it would take much to convince her. At the elevator, she blinked the burning tears from her eyes and brushed a hand to her still-sensitive lips. She could still feel him there, taste him.

She wondered whether tomorrow, her first day as a demon witch, she could say the same. Whether she would be able to think for herself at all anymore.

DARBY DIDN'T GO VERY far. Exiting the hotel's glass doors, she walked to a nearby park, her boots crunching over the snow. She waited in the quiet darkness, burrowing deep in her cloak as she sat on a park bench and watched the light snowfall with unseeing eyes.

It was cold, but she hoped that without her necklace, and in her state of utter vulnerability, a demon would find her. More than likely the same one that appeared to her in her apartment would not be too out of range to detect her. Once he found her, it would only take a few moments and the deed would be done. At least that's what she'd always been told. Warned. Whatever.

She closed her eyes in a tight, painful blink, inwardly cringing at what she was about to do. A sob built in her throat and lodged there as she thought of her aunts and how this would hurt them, devastate them. First her mother. And now her. They'd prefer her dead to this.

But she couldn't reconsider. She couldn't let anything happen to Aimee. Not if she could help it—and she could. She *would*.

It wasn't as though she were giving up on herself. It didn't have to be the end of the world for her. She could move further north and live where no demon could appear and materialize for even a moment. An environment where a demon couldn't wield control over her. She had no other choice. That's what she would have to do after this night.

The wind stirred—a chalky breeze. The snow gave off its own glow around her, a source of light in itself, a great blanket of white, radiant and bright.

She peered out from the scarf she'd wrapped several times around the lower half of her face, searching for shadows—for dark, twisted shapes that had no natural purpose on this earth. That weren't shadows at all, but something else.

Nothing. With a deep sigh, she closed her eyes and relaxed into a state that bordered sleep. She mellowed, tuning out the cold as best she could.

Her pulse slowed to a dull, rhythmic ticking at her neck, lightly hopping beneath her skin. There was no reason for her to hold herself tense and alert against bad things that might do her harm. Not when she was waiting for a demon to show up.

If she wanted to speed along the chance of that happening, then it would be better if she were in the most receptive state possible.

She'd never tried to use her gift on purpose before. Her visions simply struck her unsolicited— unwanted and reviled. But she knew witches could wield their powers. With skill and practice—neither of which she could claim—they could summon their powers at whim. Her aunts had been able to. Even her mother—she'd just been resistant.

Darby had never tried before. Now she wished she'd paid better attention to the lessons her aunts had tried to force on her.

She breathed in and out, in and out, sliding low on the bench. Her head dipped forward, her body relaxing, mind emptying, as she readied herself as much as she could for a vision.

It didn't come. This time there was no vision.

No flash of future events. Nothing to help attract a demon to her side.

But it turned out she didn't need a vision to bring a demon to her. He came to her regardless.

When she was struck with his presence, it was with such a sharp bolt of awareness that she lurched upright on the bench. In the years since she'd lived in cold climates such as this, she'd never felt a demon's presence so powerfully.

She shivered, lacing her hands tightly together as she searched for his shadow.

Maybe he came without the draw of her vision because she'd summoned him, pulling him from whatever dark beyond where he lurked. She didn't know. She'd spent her life running and hiding from demons. She didn't know what happened when you actually welcomed one with open arms.

Or maybe he came because she'd removed the necklace. Without holy water, salt and milk, she was an easier target.

She broke from the bench, still trembling as she staggered to her feet. But not from the cold. His heat was all around her, blistering her with renewed force. She hugged herself tightly and forced herself not to run.

A guttural voice taunted in her ear, the demon tongue instantly translating itself in her head.

"Now I'm almost thinking you want me here, little one, because this is simply too easy."

She turned her head slightly, angling to better view him, a shadowy shape just beginning to take form in front of her. She stiffened but showed no other sign that she was even alarmed at his presence—this thing, this shadow that was not shadow.

It was him. The same demon from before. She tried not to shudder as she gazed at his repulsive image . . . tried not to consider that this *thing* would be inside her head soon enough. That he would own her soul.

"You must like the cold," she taunted back. "You keep showing up here."

"No, I must like you," his hissing voice countered, snake's tongue darting to his nonexistent lips. "I can't seem to stay away from you."

She inhaled a difficult breath. "It seems I may need you, after all."

"Indeed?" His large snake's head nodded as though in approval.

And yet he didn't seem surprised. In fact, his slit eyes gazed down at her with a smug knowledge, like he had been waiting for this moment for a long time. She had done precisely as expected, and she wondered if there was something intrinsic to *her*. Something that marked her over other witches. Did demons know which witches would be most susceptible? Her aunts had never been particularly harassed. Not like her mother. Not like her.

It made her ill to think that she may have been headed to this moment all along—no matter how she tried, how she fought it. This was always going to happen. Always going to be.

But it wasn't over, she quickly reminded herself before despair crept over her.

This demon wasn't going to get an easy possession out of her. She'd move to Antarctica if she had to. See how much he liked that. If he wanted to use her as an instrument for evil, she wasn't going to give him a lot of opportunity to do that.

The demon continued in his slithering voice, "Well, let's proceed then." His scaly flesh shivered—shuddered, actually, and she knew he couldn't last in this temperature for much longer. "A witch's soul never comes for free. I'm aware of that. What do you want, my dear? Name your price."

She sucked in a deep breath. Nothing was more important than this moment. She had to get it right.

"There's a little girl, Aimee." She moistened her dry, cold lips. "She's been bitten by a lycan."

"Ah." The demon nodded, his serpent tongue

darting out in a way that made her stomach twist and tighten sickly. "The poor little one is infected and you want me to reverse the curse on her."

"Yes, but no tricks. I want her to be the same healthy, *human* girl she used to be. I want her returned safely to Niklas, a—" She stopped, unsure what to say about Niklas. Unsure what she should say.

What was Niklas to her? *Everything,* a small voice whispered in the back of her mind. *Everything you're losing. Everything you ever wanted and never knew.*

She swallowed against a sudden lump in her throat. The last thing she wanted this demon to think was that Niklas meant something special to her. The demon might use him to get to her when he discovered just how uncooperative she was.

"Niklas?" he prompted.

She forced her shoulders into an indifferent shrug. "Yes. He's staying at the Fairmont Hotel," she finished. "He knows the girl and will take care of her—see her safely home."

"That can all be arranged."

She stabbed a finger in his direction. "Exactly as I described," she threatened, marveling that she was even negotiating with such a hideous creature so calmly. The sight of him would have sent her running before. Before Aimee. Before Niklas.

Before she realized she couldn't spend her life running. That life was about more than her. It was about innocent little girls whose mothers were brutally murdered by monsters—a girl whose youth was ripped away, her future stolen.

It was about the fact that Darby possessed the power to give Aimee a chance at life—if she was selfless enough to do it.

The demon chuckled. "What? You don't trust me? And we're going to be so close. That hurts."

"I'm not finished."

He waved a three-taloned hand for her to continue.

"The lycan that infected her, Cyprian . . . I want him gone. Dead. Understand?" This she could do for Niklas—to say nothing of the world. But truth be told, it was mostly for Niklas. Her gift to him. He'd be free at last. What he chose to do after that, whether he devoted the rest of his life to hunting other lycans instead of living his own life for himself, was out of her hands. But this—Cyprian's wretched life—she could end it for him.

The demon counted off on his talons. "Girl returned to her old self and the lycan responsible destroyed. Sounds simple enough." He brought those creepy fingers to his scaly cheek.

Darby stared at him through narrowed eyes, replaying their agreement in her head. She remembered that Niklas's mother hadn't worded her request very well. She didn't want to repeat that mistake. After careful consideration, she gave a brisk nod. "Yes. That should do it."

The demon smiled a lipless grin. "Very good."

She tensed now, unsure what to do, how any of this happened—how the most reprehensible thing she had *never* thought to happen would actually come to pass.

"Relax, my dear. This won't hurt."

The demon stepped nearer, engulfing her in his embrace. He was uncomfortably warm. Despite the cold raging around them, his leathery flesh was baking hot. Even so, she still shivered.

"Shh." He slid his large palm across her cheek. It wasn't scaled like the rest of him, but felt rubbery and slick. "Everything's going to be all right. We'll be together forever. Just the two of us."

Bile rose to the back of her throat. This did nothing to still her trembling, but his arms tightened around her, holding her so snug she could hardly move.

"Repeat after me: I submit to you, I submit to you."

She parted her lips. The words stuck in her throat. She couldn't say it—couldn't do it. She closed her eyes, angry at herself, but a small, cowardly part of her also felt relieved.

As if he sensed this, his taunting voice filled her ears. "Don't you want to save your little girl? So innocent. So sweet. She didn't do anything to deserve what happened to her . . . what's going to happen to her. What's her name again?"

She shook her head, lips pressed tightly together.

His taloned fingers dug deep into her arms, the nails cutting her flesh. "Her name?"

Tears seeped between her closed eyelids. "Aimee."

"Ah, Aimee. Poor Aimee. Wonder how many will die at her hands. Taken in by her appearance, a lost little girl in need. She couldn't possibly harm anyone." He chuckled. "Until she devours them."

It was a horrible scenario, but one she could picture as perfectly as any vision.

She had to do this. She couldn't let that happen. The words rose on her shuddering lips: "I submit to you, I submit to you . . . I submit."

He exhaled slowly as if she had done something to ease a long-standing ache, a deeply buried wound. "It is done," he said on a breath.

Suddenly she was caught in a storm of dark wind. The demon was shadow again, steaming air swirling all around her, gaining speed until she felt like she was caught in a massive cyclone.

Suddenly the wind stopped, disappeared. And

she was slammed against something so hard every bone in her body rattled.

She was lifted off her feet and then flung back down. She lay flat on the ground, facedown in bitter-cold snow. But a strange new heat spread up from her core, suffusing her. Like something living and breathing inside her.

Looking around, there was no sight of the demon. Yet she wasn't alone. The demon was still with her. She felt him.

He was inside her.

TWENTY-FOUR

Niklas woke with a rough gasp, his heart beating like a fierce drum in his chest. Instantly, he looked around, reacquainting himself with his surroundings. One learned to do that, especially when one never woke in the same place, when the scenery constantly changed.

The fact that Darby wasn't in the room struck him immediately. His mind registered this even though his body already knew, already sensed her missing from his side.

"Darby?" he called, flinging back the covers and rising from the bed. He checked the bathroom and then the other two rooms. Scowling, he stopped, wondering where she could have gone. She wouldn't have gone looking for Aimee on her own. She needed his help for that.

He returned to his room and his gaze caught on the glint of something on the bedside table. The flesh at the back of his neck prickled. His hand trembled slightly as he reached for it, grasping the chain between his fingers. He held the necklace up and let the three charms dangle before his eyes. Darby's talisman. He'd never seen her without it.

He folded the necklace into his hand, curling his fingers into a tight fist. She left it here. He knew what that meant. Knew where she'd gone—what she'd done.

With a curse, he dropped back down on the bed and ran his fingers through his hair, tugging at the ends tightly.

Just like his mother. It was happening again. She was sacrificing herself. It felt the same. The crushing guilt. The grief.

He inhaled deeply and sat up straight. No. Not again. He wasn't going to let this happen again.

Lifting his hands, he put her necklace around his neck for safekeeping. Until he could return it to her.

Suddenly finding Cyprian wasn't nearly so important to him. He surged back to his feet, determined to find Darby. He'd already lost one woman in his life to a demon. He wasn't going to lose another one.

He dressed quickly, his mind racing, trying to imagine where Darby would have gone to do this . . . *thing*.

A soft knock sounded at the door. He paused, almost thinking he'd imagined the timid sound—until it came again.

He hurried to the door and stared out the peephole. Nothing. No one was out there. The knock came again. With a curse, and a sixth sense telling him what he would find, he yanked the door open and looked down at Aimee. She stared up at him with wide eyes in a dirt-smudged face.

Her bottom lip quivered. "I want Darby."

He squatted and swept her into his arms, hugging her close. He couldn't help thinking: *I want her, too.*

"Darby," she sobbed, burying her face in his shoulder.

He carried her into the room, making shushing sounds.

She pushed up from his shoulder, her wide eyes darting wildly around the room. "Darby! Darby!"

"Shh." Seeing no hope for it, he guided her to the couch and explained, "Honey, Darby's gone."

"Gone?" She swiped a grimy little hand against a runny nose. "Where'd she go? Who's going to take me to my grandma's? She promised she would bring me to my grandma."

"I'll do that. I'll see you get there."

Tears trailed down her cheeks in shiny tracks. "Why'd she leave me?"

"Aimee, honey, can you tell me what happened to the bad man that took you?"

"The shadows came. They got him."

"Shadows . . ." He stopped, suddenly understanding. He squeezed his eyes in a tight blink. *Demons*.

Darby did it. Of course. She'd made a pact with a demon, but not for nothing.

Cyprian was gone.

It was over. Ten years of searching, hunting, breathing and living for revenge. Done. Finished. His mother was avenged. Because of Darby.

He looked intently at Aimee. Her eyes were no longer the pewter of a lycan. She wasn't infected anymore. Darby had taken measures into her own hands. She'd sacrificed herself for Aimee. And for him.

He probed carefully inside himself, searching, testing to see if the connection to his alpha was there, if the thread that always linked them still existed.

No. Nothing. It was gone.

There was no rush of relief as he'd always expected. No sudden sense of freedom.

If anything, he was furious with himself for not guessing Darby would do something like this. And he was furious with her for sacrificing herself for Aimee. For him. Damn her.

Damn her for thinking she was somehow less important than him, that she was expendable.

She was everything. And he would show her

that—prove it to her. He'd find her. Save her as he failed to save his mother. And then he would spend every day of the rest of his life showing her just how much she meant to him. He'd show her that she didn't have to spend her life alone. That she had him. Always.

He looked down at the little girl staring up at him so expectantly. He stroked a hand over her downy-soft hair.

Aimee buried her face in his chest. "I want Darby."

"I know, sweetheart. So do I. So do I."

He'd find her. Even if it took surrendering to that part of himself that he had vowed to kill, to keep buried inside himself forever.

There was no question about what he needed to do. Darby had done the unthinkable. He could do this. He *would*.

He wouldn't lose her.

TWENTY-FIVE

It took longer than he liked to find someone to watch Aimee but he didn't want to leave the child with just anyone—not after what she'd been through. He couldn't do that to her. Or to Darby. Darby had sacrificed herself to see that Aimee was safe. He had to make sure she stayed that way.

The concierge directed him to a sweet-faced girl who worked in the gift shop. Turned out she was an art student. The moment she sat down with Aimee and began to draw pictures of zebras and teddy bears, the girl was transported to another world. Satisfied she was happy and in good hands, Niklas slipped away with no worries for her.

He left his guns behind. He knew enough about demons to know that guns wouldn't work. Just as with lycans, there were specific methods to killing demons. If he could lure the demon inside Darby out into the open, then a blade would be his only option.

He carried the weapon in his coat pocket as he

walked the quiet streets. He lifted his face to the frigid air, searching for a scent of Darby. If she was close, he could detect her. After their time together, it would be a certainty. She was in his blood now.

If he wanted more range, wanted to deepen his senses, then he would have to shift . . . have to become the hunter that burned at the core of him.

He headed through the park, where the trail of her died, vanishing into the bitterly fierce wind. He detoured off the path and found a copse of trees with snow-heavy branches that hung low, brushing the frozen earth. Ducking under the cover of those heavy branches, he stood shielded, hidden from view.

He waited, watched, peering through the latticework of frozen branches at the stillness of the park, assuring himself that no one was around. The quiet paths, the lonely benches. No one walked the park this early in the morning, especially on a day so cold. He released a resigned breath. Warm fog puffed out from his lips.

With a determined clench to his jaw, he stripped off his clothes and secured the knife to his thigh. His adrenaline pumped hard, shielding him from the worst of the cold as he stood naked, his skin tightening, pores shrinking in reaction to the freezing temperature but also in preparation for what was to come. What he willed to happen.

That warmth that was always there, simmering just beneath the surface, burst free. His veins burned hotly, his heart hammering at a frantic tempo. Air rushed from his mouth in spurts. Dipping his head, he moaned low in his throat. A scratchy, tingling sensation that bordered on pain overwhelmed his body. He threw back his head. Arched his spine. His moans grew louder and he bit his lips, not wanting to attract attention. He brought his hands to his face, clutching his cheeks. He felt his bones alter, ever so slightly stretching, pulling . . .

For once he let go, no longer struggling to hang on to himself. His emotions surged to the surface right along with the beast. He thought of Darby and the demon who had her. A red haze clouded his visions.

He couldn't stop himself. He lifted his face high to the morning wind and released a howl.

He was overwhelmed by myriad scents. Countless foods, human aromas, all manner of rotting debris from Dumpsters littering alleyways.

He sifted through the odors, hunting for one. Subtle and soft, clean as soap with an underlying hint of vanilla. It was inherently Darby and he would know it anywhere.

After several moments it was there. He found it. With a low growl in the back of his throat, he tore free from where he hid in the trees, moving so fast that the human eye would only see a blur and not his monstrous form.

His heart pounded at an unbelievable rate, matching the rhythm of his feet. He exited the park and whipped through the city, guided by his nose and instinct. Guided by his heart. Something he hadn't felt in a long time. Something he didn't think he'd ever felt.

Before Darby.

DARBY WOKE GROGGILY, HER head heavy and aching as if she were hung over from a night of binge drinking. She'd had a few of those nights in the past. When she'd first left home and everything—everyone—she ever knew, she took solace in a bottle once or twice. Until mornings like this convinced her to stop feeling sorry for herself and put an end to that.

The cold greeted her stiff body. With a wince, she lifted her face, peeling it off a grimy surface. The entire side of her body that pressed against the floor ached. Tears pricked her eyes as blood flowed back into those numb parts of her body. With the flow of blood came pain.

She contemplated her situation as she blinked her burning eyes. The demon must have grown tired of the struggle—with her and the bitter cold.

She carefully prodded around inside herself, poking about to see if he was somewhere in there, just dormant. Did demons even sleep? She didn't sense him at all. Not inside her or anywhere else.

Faint memories of the night before filtered through her mind. She concentrated, pulling them forth like elusive dreams from the dark.

It had been a constant battle throughout the night between her and the demon. Back and forth they went. One moment she would wrest control when the demon slipped away, too plagued by the cold.

In those moments of freedom, she would walk as quickly as she could, practically running from the bus station where he'd been trying to lead her. And she didn't need an explanation as to why he was taking her there. He was trying to get her on a bus headed south, where it wasn't so cold. If he succeeded in that, she would forever be at his mercy. Her face felt tight and itchy with the weight of this very real fear.

Slowly and with a hiss of discomfort, she rose into a sitting position, taking a moment to assess her surroundings. She didn't know where she was. In a building of some sort, on the floor of a dingy room where the overriding color was gray. Faint sunlight trickled in from the boarded-up windows, motes of dust dancing on the beams.

In the distance a car alarm blared over the cacophony of a relentless power drill. She pushed the tangle of red hair from her face and inspected her room more fully. Newspaper littered the floor. It dawned on her that this was an abandoned house that transients probably used. She had somehow found her way here during the night.

Standing, she stretched out her sore muscles and rubbed filthy hands on the thighs of her jeans. God, she felt gross. It felt necessary. She needed to find a bathroom and get washed up. She doubted she could even get on a bus looking the way she did.

But she needed to hurry. Her demon could come back at any moment. *Her* demon. Her stomach rolled, rebelling against the sour thought. That her life had fallen to such lows, that *she* had fallen to such depths rocked her to her core.

For Aimee . . . for Niklas, a voice whispered across her mind. That made it worth it. Aimee was safe now. And Niklas would have peace at last. They'd forget her and move on with their lives.

Strange that this had all happened just when she'd opened herself up for the first time in her life. Just when she had decided to embrace people back into her life. *Love*—when she had thought to try to find love for herself again. That maybe she deserved it like everyone else. That she needed it to live through this life.

Her newly woken legs shook as she strode to one of the boarded windows. A big crack gaped between the nailed-up boards. She wanted to get a glimpse of the world waiting for her.

She peered outside. The face of a brownstone apartment building stared back at her from across the street. A construction site was in full swing next door to it. Several men with hard hats walked in and out of the structure, carrying boards, wiring and other materials. Maybe she could ask one of them for directions to the bus station—where she would buy a ticket for the first bus headed north.

Turning, she exited the room and entered a narrow hallway. Dim and airless, hardly any light penetrated it. Without any windows, it felt as if she had suddenly stepped into night. She put a hand to the wall and felt her way along, skimming the ripped plaster with trailing fingers. In the murky air, she detected what looked like a descending staircase at the far end. She made her way carefully, shivering in the cold, stale space.

She hardly noticed the change in the air at first. It was insidious, a subtle thread of warm air drifting and curling around her ankles, then easing up each calf. The heat expanded, a pleasant thing in this bitter cold. But still she shivered. It could mean only one thing. There could only be one source for the sudden heat.

Glancing down, her eyes rapidly scanned the area around her, registering only the murky gloom that pervaded the length of the corridor. The demon's dark shadow might be hard to see, but she didn't need sight to know he was here, that her demon had returned to claim her again.

She sensed him, felt him. Knew him as she knew herself.

Panic clawed up her throat. She turned, ready to run, flee. Where, she didn't know. She wasn't thinking rationally. She only knew she had to keep running.

A sudden crash sounded behind her and she risked a glance over her shoulder. A cry strangled in her throat at the sight that greeted her.

A lycan stood at the top of the stairs, all heaving muscle and sinew. Her first thought was Cyprian—until she recalled that he was dead now. That had been the deal. And upon further inspection, she saw that he looked nothing like Cyprian. He even held himself differently. Legs spaced apart in an oddly familiar way.

His eyes glowed across the distance at her. A bright, burning light within a sea of indigo.

Her pulse stuttered against her throat. "Niklas?"

She took a sliding step toward him, still uncertain. Niklas would never shift, never surrender to that part of himself. He'd made that abundantly clear.

He moved toward her, sinew rippling beneath bronze fur. He growled low in his throat, a noise that sounded suspiciously like her name. And there were those eyes again, drilling into her with familiar intensity.

"Niklas!" She surged forward. He'd found her! He'd come for her . . .

A dark wind swirled between them in the corridor, the hot air singeing her skin, reminding her that they weren't alone.

"Niklas!" she cried, stretching out a hand as if she could reach him—or push him away. The impulses to do each warred within her. "Go! Run away, Niklas! It's too late for me! Get out of here!"

His response was to pull a deadly-looking blade from a strap attached to his thigh. With a shout, he charged at the demon's hazy shape.

"Niklas, no!" she screamed.

He didn't stand a chance fighting a demon that was nothing more than shadow. Only she could see him—only witches and the rare few demon slayers.

And the only way a demon could be killed is through locating the mark of the fall on him and stabbing him there. An impossibility when Niklas could see only the vague, shadowy shape of him. Darby knew this. Niklas knew this, too. And yet he was here. Fighting an impossible battle for her. Why?

She supposed it should have thrilled her that he would do such a brave, reckless thing for her. And maybe some part of her was thrilled—but for the most part she was just terrified. She hadn't sacrificed herself just to get Niklas killed, and that was what was going to happen if he didn't leave.

"Niklas!" she shrieked. "Go! Get out of here!"

Niklas ignored her, swiping and plunging his blade into the demon's writhing and swirling shape.

The demon flashed a grin of razor-sharp teeth. Evidently he enjoyed toying with Niklas and was in no hurry to take possession of her.

She wrung her hands in helplessness, felt despair squeeze her heart dry. At least the demon couldn't harm Niklas—not while he was still a shadow. Cold realization washed over her then. *But he could.*

He could harm Niklas. He could kill him— *through her.* If he took possession of her, which he'd been about to do before Niklas showed up, he could then destroy Niklas.

Her eyes ached as she watched the scene play out before her—Niklas fighting what he couldn't see and her nasty demon relishing every moment of it. It was only a matter of time before her demon tired of the game and claimed her. And then it would be all over. Niklas would be dead.

She shook her head firmly, every muscle in her body tightening and pulling taut. She couldn't let that happen—couldn't let herself be used that way. Couldn't let a demon manipulate her into killing the man she loved.

The man she loved.

At any other time this realization would have given her pause—would have left her shaken and reeling. But there wasn't time for that.

She scanned the narrow hall, as if she could find a way out that wasn't there before. Nothing. There was no way she could break past the demon and Niklas to the stairs. She was going to have to find another way out.

As Niklas attacked her demon, came at him again and again, she inched back down the hall and plunged into the room where she'd spent the night. She attacked the boarded-up window with both hands, clawing at the boards until her nails cracked and bled. Still, she didn't stop. Anxious breath sawed from her lips as she worked in a frenzy to escape.

She had managed to get one board free when she felt the hot sweep of air blow into the room.

With a gasp, she spun around, her hands flattening against the window behind her, heedless of the sharp, rusted nails scratching her palms. Apparently the demon had tired of Niklas and decided to end things.

The demon swept toward her on a hot cyclone of air. His serpent eyes honed in on her with hard intent.

Niklas was there, too. Just behind him—all raging lycan, a beast frightening in his wrath, slicing his blade after the demon as if he might actually do some lasting damage with it.

"Niklas, stop! Go get out of here!"

He ignored her, stabbing blindly with his knife, making contact with the demon but never in the correct spot. The demon hissed in annoyance as Niklas struck him in the arm, tearing his flesh. Green blood so dark it was almost black welled from the wound before the flesh sealed itself, healing up again.

Darby squinted and scanned his scaled flesh, hoping she might be able to identify the mark somewhere on the demon and relate to Niklas where to strike. It was a desperate, unlikely hope.

And no, she couldn't see it anywhere. Bleakness welled up inside her as the demon lifted himself high off the ground and then came at her, flying full force into her.

It was like getting hit by a truck. The impact stunned her, left her dazed. She felt herself slipping away, being pushed under, dragged, dragged down, somewhere far away. Almost like she was submerged in a pool of warm water and being held under. She tried to swim to the surface and break free. To take that huge gulp of breath to freedom. But she couldn't. She was trapped, a prisoner inside herself.

Niklas, she thought. *Please, get out of here. Leave while you can.* And then she thought no more.

TWENTY-SIX

Niklas knew the precise moment he lost Darby. The demon's shadowy shape faded from the room—there was no sign of the bastard anymore. Niklas was left facing Darby. And yet not Darby.

He growled, the sound vibrating from deep inside his chest as he gazed into her eyes. Hazel no more. They were a soulless black, the whites obliterated.

"Well, lycan," the demon sneered in Darby's voice. A strange thing to hear her voice and know it wasn't her. "Where do we go from here?"

He knew precisely where the demon wanted him to go. He wanted him to attack Darby—kill her so that he could then be free. If a demon witch was killed, the demon was released. It was the only way a demon could take corporeal form and walk freely on earth.

Niklas flexed the knife in his clawed hand and inhaled. He wasn't idiot enough to be led down that path. No, what he needed to do was get that demon back out of Darby so he could finish him off.

"You care about the witch, do you?" Demon-Darby cocked her head, sending her red hair tossing over one shoulder. "How singular . . . for a lycan." He released a throaty laugh. "Then you should spare her. Put her out of her misery. If you care about her, you won't leave her like this." Using Darby's elegant hands, the demon motioned to her body, which he inhabited.

"Stop hiding behind her and come out and fight, you coward," Niklas said thickly, his voice almost unintelligible.

"Didn't we just do that? It was so . . . tedious. You stabbing over and over, never even scratching me." He sighed, but Niklas noticed he shivered, too. The cold was getting to him. He couldn't hang on much longer.

Niklas smiled. "Cold, isn't it?"

Demon-Darby scowled and lifted a hand. The mere motion was all it took to send Niklas flying and crashing back into the wall. The force jarred him to his very bones and he had to resist the impulse to attack. He held himself in check. One look at Darby's face was all it took. He'd never harm her as long as she was in there, somewhere. If he went after the demon, it would be Darby taking the hit.

The bastard wanted that. He wanted Niklas to kill Darby. Because once that happened, he would be free. Once her body was broken, he could come out. No longer a shadow. No longer with his hands tied. He would be set loose on the world and wreak whatever damage he chose.

Demon-Darby flexed her fingers. "Oh, that felt good. Let's do that again."

Niklas staggered to his feet, bracing himself for the next attack as Darby approached. She lifted her hand and blasted Niklas with a second rush of air. He resisted it for a moment, managed to stay on his feet, and then he was flying through the air again, helpless against the force of the current.

The demon made a tsking sound, cocking Darby's head and sending her magnificent hair tossing around her shoulders. "Shame. I didn't expect this to end so quickly, but as you said, it is rather cold here. I can't afford to dally any longer." He glanced around then. "I suppose I'll have to leave Darby here again. Like last night. Only this time, when she wakes, it will be to find you dead beside her."

It was a strange sensation, staring at the face of the woman he loved and feeling only loathing. Because it wasn't Darby. He wasn't dealing with the woman he loved right now.

Yes. He loved Darby. The realization that he

loved her slid through him smoothly, without the slightest ripple. It should have struck him as a surprise, but it didn't. Why else would he be here if he didn't love her?

Fresh resolve coursed through him. Thinking only of doing what he could to drive the demon from Darby's body, he reached for the necklace at his throat—Darby's necklace—and ripped it free.

Before the demon could react, he moved in a blur of speed. He pressed the necklace deep into her throat, just below her collarbone. He held it there, pressed against her flesh, hoping that combined with the cold it was enough of an irritant to send the demon running.

The demon shrieked and thrashed, but Niklas clung to Darby, pulling her close to him, holding the three charms tightly against her skin no matter how she fought him.

"Come on, Darby, come back to me," he urged in a whisper, staring into her still-black eyes.

"No," the demon spat. "She's mine now. And forever."

"Wrong." With a final push, he drove the charms hard enough against her flesh to shatter each of the vials. They broke from the fierce pressure. He felt the liquid from within roll between his fingers and onto her skin, along with the gritty slide of the salt.

As each charm cracked open, holy water, salt and milk did their damage. The instant the three elements hit her, tendrils of smoke lifted off the surface of her skin, but he didn't let go.

Even as he hated that he was hurting her, he knew that there was no help for it. The wound would heal and she'd be right in the end . . . as long as he managed to kill her demon.

Darby's throat arched, the tendons stretched in agony.

Satisfaction curled through him as her eyes began to fade, flashing in and out. Soulless black one moment and hazel the next.

"Let her go," he growled, shaking her, his clasp on her neck scalding hot. He knew his Darby was there, close to the surface.

A moan spilled from her lips. The sound came from her. It was Darby. He knew it.

Then he was blown free, ripped from her arms as the demon burst from her in a swirl of black shadow. Niklas's blade flew from his hand and clattered to the ground.

Darby collapsed a few feet from him in a limp, boneless pile. Niklas scrambled toward her, carefully lifting her with his beastly hands.

The demon roared above them in a violent circling wind. Niklas held Darby close, shielding her, protecting her, telling himself the demon would leave now. That he wouldn't dare come at her again. Not right now. This was over. For now. It had to be.

Turning so that his cheek pressed against Darby's hair, he gazed at the window Darby had tried to escape through. He stared at the beams of sunlight, marveling that the sun could be shining at all right now. He was convinced that the sun would never shine again if he lost Darby.

DARBY CRACKED HER BLEARY eyes, the same fuzziness as before clogging her head. Would it be this way every time her demon took possession? Would she come to, struggling to recollect, to recall the horrors she'd committed at the behest of a demon?

Soft fur surrounded her. Her gaze slid up and she gasped at the lycan staring down at her—until she saw his eyes. Until she remembered. *Niklas*.

She tilted her face closer to look upon him, and the motion made her cringe. Her neck burned, stung like fire. She lightly touched the raw, scorched flesh there.

Dark wind swirled all around them, lifting trash, debris and newspaper into the air like wild birds. The demon's outraged cries pummeled her ears. She flung her hands up to try and block out the sound.

Through the haze she could see him clearly. He tore through the air around them, his hideous face twisted in fury. He wasn't done with her. With them. His rage fed him, made him stronger, strong enough to withstand the cold a little longer.

He was going to have another go at her. She knew it, felt it inside herself, in that part that was now linked to him.

She turned, sought Niklas's face. Smiling, she reached up to touch him, stroke him, unafraid at the sight of him. If this was it, the end, it wasn't so bad that it happened while in his arms. A month ago, she had no one to hold her.

Now she had him.

She'd beat out her mother's prediction. She wasn't alone. He had shifted for her. *For her*. She didn't think anyone had ever done such a thing for her before. And to stay here even when it meant he would die. She'd never had that before. Someone who cared enough. Who loved her. Looking into his eyes, she saw that. Knew it to be true.

As much as she wanted him to go, to leave her, to be all right someplace safe far away from her, her heart felt warm and full in a way it had never felt before.

He smiled back at her, or rather grimaced. She doubted he could truly smile as a lycan, but she knew he meant to smile.

Drained and tired from her recent possession, she felt her hand fall limply from his face. She was too weak to even hold it up any longer.

"You should go," she whispered over the roar of wind and shadow. She had to try. At least one more time.

Her hand brushed something cold and metallic on the ground.

"I'm not leaving you," he responded in his thick, guttural voice. An animal's voice that would make anyone else shrink in terror. Or run. But she knew the man underneath. The soul within.

She felt the ground, patting with her hand. Her fingers closed around the object, identifying it. *Niklas's knife*. She tested the weight of it, surprisingly light in her hand. The handle felt abrasive against her palm but good, reassuring in its solidness.

She looked away from Niklas, fixing her gaze on the demon she'd been afraid to look at. He held himself over her in a state of full wrath, his slit eyes spitting fury, his lipless mouth curled in a snarl.

"You'll regret giving me so much trouble," he uttered in his ancient tongue, the words instantly translating in her mind.

He arched himself high above her, preparing to plunge back inside her. And in that moment it would be over. Everything done. The air locked in her lungs as she braced for it.

Niklas wouldn't leave. There was no use begging. She couldn't make him go. He was as stubborn and determined as she was. So he would stay—and her demon would see him dead through her, manipulating her.

And that's when she saw it. The mark of the fall where he was pushed from Heaven. The sign of God's abandonment. His Achilles' heel, nestled in deep shadow under his biceps. A thin handprint glowed brightly, beckoning her. *She saw it!*

Her heart skipped, stuttered and then took off in a wild beat. Before she could think or even wonder if she could do it—if she could manage it—she lurched off the ground and plunged the blade deep into the demon's vulnerable flesh just as he was descending.

His scream filled the air. A hellish screech that could shatter glass. Darby brought her hands to her ears. Niklas held her tightly, and together they watched as the demon clawed at the blade, trying to pull it free of his scaled gladiator body. But it was too late. She'd made contact—wounded him in the one place he could never heal.

The demon crumpled, wilted before her eyes, blurring into a twisting plume of smoke as he dropped to the floor. Gradually the air cleared, leaving nothing. No sign of the demon that had once possessed her.

Gasping and shaking, she fell back down to the ground. Niklas caught her up in his arms.

"Darby!" He shifted then, returned to himself. She was instantly surrounded by smooth, warm muscle. He slid a familiar callused palm along her cheek. She smiled faintly as she realized she wasn't the only one shaking. "You did it!"

She nodded, the motion as jerky and erratic as her pulse. "You came," she whispered, gazing into his indigo eyes. "You shifted."

He grinned, one corner of his mouth cocking in that way that made her breath fall faster. "It was nothing."

She swatted his bare shoulder. Transitioning, shifting into that thing, that part of himself which he hated . . . it had been everything. And she knew it.

She peered intently at his face. "I wouldn't be free if it wasn't for you. I won't ever forget what you did for me today. For Aimee. It was brave— stupid, but brave." Then a thought dawned on her. "Aimee!" she exclaimed. "Where is she? She was supposed to return to you—"

"She's fine. She's being watched by a very nice lady back at the hotel. We'll go see her right now."

She relaxed, nodding. Of course, Niklas would see that Aimee was safe.

He sobered. His touch on her cheeks grew firmer, the pressure of each finger searing. "Why do you make it sound like you're going somewhere? Like this is good-bye?"

"I—" She didn't know what to say to that. She shivered, and remembered herself and where they were, what had just happened. Staring into his eyes, she could forget everything. "We better get out of here. It's cold."

"Nice change of subject. But you're not running out on me." He shook his head, slowly, his devouring gaze never wavering from her face. "Not ever again."

Her chest grew tight and itchy from the way he was looking at her. She swallowed and moistened her lips as the words in her heart rose up on her lips. "I don't want to leave you, Niklas. I didn't want to leave you back at the hotel—"

"But you did."

"Because I had to."

"You *thought,* inaccurately, that you had to." His hand slid around to grip the back of her head. "Don't ever do that to me again." His voice softened, gentled to almost a plea. "Okay?"

She nodded, emotion thickening her throat.

He pressed a kiss to her lips, speaking as he did so, "Now let's go home."

Home. God, that word sounded good. For

the first time in a long time, it felt real. It felt possible. It didn't occur to her to wonder where home was. Because she knew, with blinding certainty, that her home was with him and it always would be.

TWENTY-SEVEN

Darby and Niklas stared through the lightly falling snow at the pretty little house with gingerbread trim. It was something out of a storybook. In the emerging day smoke curled from the brick chimney. A beautiful piece of stained glass hung in the large front bay window. A cat appeared in the windowsill, stretching so that its calico tail brushed the framed glass.

Darby rubbed her hand up and down Aimee's slight arm. "This is the place," she announced. There was only one Alice Davies listed as a resident of this town.

"I remember the pretty glass in the window." Aimee pointed at the house, leaning forward anxiously. "And that's Patch. I remember he used to chew my toes." She giggled and the sound lifted Darby's heart.

Darby smiled, glad to see her anxious to reunite with her grandmother, but sad, too. Sad to say good-bye. She slid a lock of soft brown hair behind the girl's ear.

Aimee looked at her, some of the happiness dimming from her eyes. "Don't you want to come in with me?"

Darby slid a pained glance at Niklas. They'd gone over this. She knew it was the only way. His look was sympathetic, even as his eyes conveyed what she already knew. Aimee had to go in alone.

With a deep breath, she drew the girl into her arms and hugged her tightly. "No. We can't go with you, honey."

"Aimee," Niklas began, his voice gentle. "You know it's not a good idea to tell anyone what happened—"

"You mean about the monsters?"

Niklas flicked his gaze to Darby, questioning, unsure whether he should confirm this. Darby gave him an encouraging nod. They couldn't erase any of the things from Aimee's mind.

"Yes. The monsters. It's not a good idea to tell people about them—"

"Yeah. No one would believe me." Aimee nodded, her blue-green eyes widely innocent but also wise beyond her years.

"Probably not," he agreed.

"They'd probably think I was loony."

"Yes," Darby quickly inserted. "And we wouldn't want them to think you're loony."

"They could lock me up in the loony bin." She nodded solemnly, and Darby was surprised at how unerringly close to the truth that statement was.

"Yes," Darby agreed, solemn in turn.

She wrinkled her little nose. "And you know, I don't really want to talk about them anymore. I'd rather forget them."

"I can understand that. You've been a very brave girl."

Aimee gathered her small bag of things, her movements reflecting her eagerness to be on her way, to see her grandmother. Darby forced her hands to remain still at her sides, letting her go. She should be glad it's this easy for the girl. She had endured a lot. Darby didn't want her sad or reluctant to leave. No sense this being hard for both of them.

With one hand on the latch of the car door, Aimee stopped and turned, smiling back at Darby. Darby felt herself smile back, even though her heart was aching.

Aimee flung herself into Darby's arms one final time. As if sensing Darby's sadness, she said, "It's going to be all right, Darby. I have Gram. She'll take care of me." She pulled back and looked into Darby's face with those wise eyes. "And you have Niklas."

Darby nodded, finding no difficulty agreeing with that statement. Her gaze slid to him and her heart swelled. She had Niklas.

Then Aimee was gone, out the door and running up the snow-covered walk. Darby could hear her pounding on the front door from where they sat inside the car. A middle-aged woman opened the door, her expression startled to find Aimee standing there by herself. But joy was soon there, eclipsing any other emotion. The woman bent down and hugged Aimee, looking as though she would never let her go.

Darby watched, breathless, bittersweet happiness filling her chest as Aimee and her grandmother went inside the house.

"Well," Niklas said, letting the finality of that word hang on the air for a moment. "You did it. You got her home safely."

"We did it," she corrected. A lump formed in her throat. They were done here. Darby had kept her promises to Aimee.

And her promise to herself. To open herself to life. To open her heart.

Rather than get out of the car, Darby climbed into the front seat and dropped down beside Niklas. She covered his hand with her own and wove her fingers through his.

Her head fell back against the headrest. His

eyes slid over her, lazy and seductive, warming her from the inside out. "Ready?" he asked.

"For anything," she returned with a coy smile, buckling herself in.

"Oh, really?" He leaned across the distance separating them and kissed her, pressing his warm lips over hers until the kiss grew into something hungry and deep. When he broke free, she was breathless and wanting more.

His smile was blinding, gorgeous and genuine, the grooves on either side of his cheeks deep.

"You have me," he said, echoing Aimee's earlier comment.

"That's right." It was more than she had ever hoped, ever dreamed she would have.

"And I have you." His hand turned over, his palm kissing hers. With one hand on the wheel, he guided them out onto the road. They weren't alone anymore. They had each other.

She looked back once to the cozy house with its smoking chimney, and then looked ahead again. The sun was starting to come out, breaking through the clouds. Suddenly the road looked very bright.

Turning, she looked at Niklas, catching his gaze, basking in the warmth of his smile, in the happiness of her heart.

Everything looked brighter.

EXPLORE THE
DARK SIDE OF DESIRE
with bestselling Paranormal Romance from Pocket Books!